A Spooky Irish Tale
for Children

A SPOOKY IRISH TALE
FOR CHILDREN

EDDIE LENIHAN

MERCIER PRESS

MERCIER PRESS
PO Box 5, 5 French Church Street, Cork
16 Hume Street, Dublin 2

© Eddie Lenihan 1996

A CIP is available for this book from the British Library

ISBN 1 85635 150 5

10 9 8 7 6 5 4 3 2 1

TO THE SECOND YEAR STUDENTS OF COLÁISTE FCJ, CNOC AN LABHRAS, LIMERICK, WHOSE ADVICE AS TO THE LIKES AND DISLIKES OF YOUNG READERS WAS MOST HELPFUL

Printed in Ireland by Colour Books Ltd.

IN IRELAND, AT THE TIME OF THE FIANNA, painting was an unknown art. In any banqueting-hall, of even the most wealthy chieftain, the walls were bare. White and bare. And very clean they looked, too – at least until the huge mid-winter feasts, when crowds of guests would soon change their colour by standing against them scratching their rumps for want of better entertainment. But the solution was simple and time-honoured: flake up another coat of whitewash and all would be as good as new.

In no hall were pictures to be found. The people of Ireland, in fact, had no glimmer of a notion what a picture even was. But that lack worried them not at all. They were well satisfied with their bare walls since they knew no better.

Now, Fionn MacCumhail was a most friendly man and whenever he found himself walking the roads and byways of Ireland he liked nothing better than some company to pass the miles. He had it, too, in his dogs Bran and Sceolaing, but even Fionn could get tired of talking to dogs, in spite of the fact that they could understand his every word and do everything except answer him back. This fact was a great loss to him and a mighty incentive for him to seek out the company of any person, stranger or otherwise, he met with on his travels. Sometimes, naturally, he made mistakes and fell in with people he would have been well content never to have met at all, but usually those he talked to were interesting and widened out his knowledge of the world, be it by ever so little.

One day Fionn was returning from a short visit to King Cormac's great forest in Lár na hÉireann. He had been sent from Tara by his royal master to check that the trees and game-animals were still there, for the men of that part of the kingdom had the strange belief that they had every bit as much right to these things as the king himself. That was a notion that Cormac was trying his best to discourage, so the Fianna were sent several times a year – always unannounced – to make sure that all was as it should be. The thievery never stopped fully, of course, but it was of no great consequence since no man was prepared to be caught in the act by Fionn or his comrades. If that happened his best move would be to arrange a swift passage out of Ireland and a long stay in distant parts. Fionn was known to be ungentle with stealers above all other wrongdoers: 'The man that'll face me, I'll half respect him even though he's trying to take the eye out of my head. But let him beware who creeps up behind my back to do me harm. That man is maimed for life when I put my hand on him.'

He meant every word of it, too.

On the day in question, while returning from the royal forest, Fionn fell into conversation with an odd-looking fellow at the cross-roads of Cluain na Lobhar. The man was standing, looking this way and that, as if undecided which road to take, when he noticed Fionn. At once his face brightened.

'It is I who am glad to see someone like your noble self,' he beamed. 'A great mystery it was to me which road I might walk upon from here. Can you be so kind as to tell me?'

'Well, begor,' said Fionn, thrown somewhat by his unusual accent, 'I could, maybe, if I knew where you wanted to go.'

'Ah, it matters not. No, not even a small bit. All roads are maybe good. Or bad.'

His accent certainly *was* odd; Fionn noticed that at once. But there was something else too that made him peer closer at this character: his words did not seem to make a great deal of sense. Was he drunk? Or astray in his mind? It would be very poor manners indeed to ask immediately the questions he wanted answers to – Who are you? Where are you from? What's your business here? – but the traveller seemed to read his mind, for with a little laugh he said: 'I see many puzzles in your eyes, big man, like where do I come from. And that I can answer, but not some of the others you wish to know.'

'Well, I s'pose that's a start,' said Fionn. 'Talk away, so, an' I'll put no word crossways to you until you finish.'

'Have your ears ever heard of the land of Germany?'

'No,' said Fionn. 'At least I don't ... But hold on! Yes. They have. Indeed they have. I was never in it but I passed close by it, I'd say, the time myself an' the Fianna were following the black footprints to Transylvania. Sure, aren't the two places nearly next-door to each other.' Knowledge of the geography of the big world outside of Ireland had never been a strong point with Fionn. But he was smiling now, at the fond memory of that great adventure and so did not notice the man looking oddly at him. He continued, 'an' d'you know, everyone we met during that journey had the same story: that 'tis full of big rivers, dark forests an' very wild people.'

The man's head jerked up and with blazing eyes he shouted: 'Wrong they are! As wrong as wrong can be. Why do all who visit that beautiful country see it with eyes of darkness only? It is hateful to me when men talk like so.'

He was excited. That much was very clear, whatever might be the reason. But Fionn answered quietly, eyeing him closely now.

'Look! Don't mind getting hot about it. I'm only telling you what I heard, an' if you don't like it that's nothing to do with me.'

'Ah, but it has, my friend.'

Fionn did not much like his tone of voice.

'Hold on a minute, now, me lad. I don't know where you get the idea that I'm your friend. I never before laid eyes on you. So, look, why don't you go that road there?' – pointing him to the left – 'There's sure to be something fierce interesting at the end of it.'

'Like the sea,' he added in his own mind.

'No, no. I will go no road now except with you. I know that you are the one who has been sent to guide me.'

'That's where you're very wrong,' growled Fionn. 'If I need company I'll pick it myself. So bye bye, an' I hope you find whatever it is you're after.'

But the man would have none of it.

'You are the one. Nothing else matters to me now. Where you go I must follow.'

Fionn did his best over the next few minutes to persuade his new 'friend' to take another road, but he might as well have been talking to the fields for all the notice he took. It even entered his mind once to strike him. But the man was unarmed.

Unarmed? The oddness of it only now began to register with him. He paused. Such a thing was unusual. No traveller went unarmed unless a slave or a madman. And he certainly had not the appearance of a slave, whatever else. In fact, as Fionn looked closer at him it became more obvious that he was a man of some refinement. He held himself well and spoke clearly, too, even if his accent grated on the ear and none of what he had to say was very welcome to Fionn. He had better investigate further, he decided, if only to be on the safe side.

'Tell me again, where did you say you were from?'

'I did not say.'

'But didn't you mention Germany?'

'Yes. But only to ask if you had heard of it.'

'All right, so,' said Fionn, 'where *are* you from?'

'From Germany.'

Fionn's lips twitched. He was not amused. This fellow was trying to be smart, was playing games with him.

'Look, boyo. If you want to be funny, go somewhere else. It isn't a healthy place around here. I heard stories many a time of funny lads disappearing into bogholes an' never again being heard about.' And he turned away, gruffly.

The man stood blinking for a moment, then started after him.

'Funny? How have I been funny? Please tell me, what have I done? Why are you angry with me?'

Fionn kept walking. Better to leave him there. Even to reply would only cause more bother. But he was gone no more than six strides when he was stopped in his tracks by: 'Big man, it is no good to run away. You must take me to meet the king of this land. I have important words to tell him.'

Fionn turned. 'Who's running away? Me, is it? I never ran from any man, never mind from a weed like you, an' ... '

He was not allowed to finish.

'It is a serious matter to speak so to the messenger to a king. You know that?'

Fionn considered. Was this fellow genuine or merely playing for time? Again he was interrupted.

'Observe, my friend. You think I am mad to travel these roads with no weapons, eh?'

'I do,' snapped Fionn, 'even though we have a fine peaceful country here; the best in the world, I'd say.'

'Ah, but I did not know that – if it is true.'

There it was again, that tone of voice that made Fionn feel so much like clouting him. But he restrained himself.

'You can believe me, 'tis true, all right. An' d'you know why?'

The man merely smiled.

'Because I'm here to make sure it stays that way.'

'Ah,' he nodded, seemingly interested. 'And what is your name, can I ask?'

'You can. I'm Fionn MacCumhail, first servant to Cormac, king of all Ireland.'

'So. I have heard much telling of you. And your men – what you call your Fianna, is that so?'

'You have it. An' now, as protector of this road, I'm asking you what are you doing standing on it.'

Fionn smiled grimly. If this lad wanted to play at being smart so could he.

'I have told you. I am come to speak to the king. Cormac, you say his name is.'

'For what?'

'Ah. That is business for his ears only. But this much I can reveal. You see that I have no weapons?'

Fionn nodded.

'Yet I am protected.'

'How so?' growled Fionn, suspicious. 'Is it spells an' the works of magic that keep you safe? Are you a druid?'

He smiled.

'No. I have heard of them, and of the druids of Ireland especially. But I am not of them.'

'Are you a rat-charmer, so?'

'No.'

'Or a ciaróg-doctor?'

'Not I.'

'Was your mother a bean feasa or your father a gruagach?'

'I do not think so.'

'Well, sure, you're a harmless creature, so, an' how could you protect yourself against the wild things that wander the roads of the world?'

'In this bag my power is,' smiled the man, slipping a pack from his back. Fionn looked at it closely. It was not large, just an ordinary-looking traveller's pack, made from some kind of animal-skin. The fur was still on it and a thong bound it at the neck. There was nothing to indicate what it might contain.

'While I carry this no harm can come to any but my enemies and to those who try to do me hurt.'

Fionn could believe that. Had he not his own oxter-bag to prove the truth of it? And, by Crom, strange were the things that had leaped out of that same bag to help him in moments of danger.

'Tell me this,' he said, more friendly than before. 'Can you take what you like out of it, or do you just stick in your hand an' hope for the best?' He was curious to know if it was similar to his own model.

'I do not understand,' replied the man. 'What ... ?'

'Look,' said Fionn, dragging round his bag from beneath his right oxter, 'if I stick my hand into this, there's no knowing what'll come out. Maybe even only half of my fingers.'

'Ah, so you are an artist too. But I do not know what you speak of about your hand. When I open this bag I know exactly what will be there. Look!' – and he proceeded to empty its contents.

Out of it came another bag, this one flat, like a wallet, and also tied with a thong. He placed it carefully to one side and began to display the other items within, for all the world like a stall-owner setting up shop in a market-place. And what he had to show was a collection of two dozen or more little stone jars, all the same size but distinguished one from another by a blob of colour at the top. And such colours! Fionn had never seen so many. But something else was bothering him.

'What was it you called me there a minute ago?' he asked carefully. The man paused, shrugged.

'Called you? I do not remember calling you anything,' and he continued his busy arranging of his wares.

'But you did,' insisted Fionn. 'A word I never heard before, either.' The man stopped and cocked his head, thinking.

'Ah! Now I recall. I said you were an artist too, no?'

'That's the word I was looking for. Now, what does it mean?' Neither Fionn nor any other of the men of Ireland had met such a person before so the word had never entered their ears.

The man sat, looked steadily at Fionn a moment and then looked away quickly. He did not reply at once, as if he were considering something. Fionn became impatient.

'Come on! I can't wait here all day. What's an artist? I hope 'tisn't something dishonourable you're calling me.'

'Not at all,' the man laughed. 'On the contrary, indeed. It is a name of honour – and power.'

'Well, I'll take your word for it, but you still didn't tell me what it means.'

'It means someone who makes pictures. Like me.'

From Fionn's puzzled blinking it was at once obvious to the artist that he was still far from understood.

'Can it really be that no one paints in Ireland?'

Fionn shook his head.

'But surely, your walls, your rooms ... you do not leave them bare, do you?'

Fionn brightened. 'Aha! Now I know what you mean. Sure, of course we do the walls. Whitewash we call it in this country. Though, by Crom, you wouldn't think 'twas very white if you saw it at the end of a big feast. You'd swear some of them animals don't wash themselves from one end of the year to ....' and he wandered on happily into reminiscences while the artist gaped at him as if he had lost every shred of his sanity. At last Fionn finished and, more at ease now, he offered to bring the artist to Tara, promising that the king would surely wish to meet someone who could brighten the place up.

The man seemed impatient about something but resigned to let Fionn chatter on if that was what it took to be introduced to the king. And so they started for Tara. But they were gone only a short distance when Fionn stopped abruptly.

'Tell me,' he said, 'how much would you charge, now, if I asked you to paint my walls at home?'

'Nothing,' snapped the artist, very coldly, a thing that Fionn seemed not to notice.

'Aw, now, I wouldn't expect you to do the job for nothing. A man has to live, too, whatever about being neighbourly an' obliging.'

'I charge nothing,' said the man icily, 'because I do *not* whitewash walls.'

'But aren't you just after saying ...'

'No, I am not. Why cannot you listen instead of always talking, big man? I said I am an artist. One who paints.'

'An' I heard you clear enough saying it. But what else would you be painting except walls? You'd hardly go putting whitewash on the floor.' Fionn laughed at this little joke, but the artist merely looked bored.

'I will make it very simple for you, large person. I do not paint walls. What I paint is people, trees, grass, the sky – the whole world,' and he spread his arms wide as he said it. 'All that you can see. But I do not paint walls – except when no other work is to be got and I must eat. Painting walls is a task for servants only.'

Fionn was mystified and well his face showed it. He stood a few moments, head to one side, scratching his beard, trying hard to understand. But to no avail.

'Yerra, 'tis trying to fool me you are. Sure, why would anyone want to paint grass? Isn't green enough of a colour for it? Or what would a person want paint on himself for? That don't make no sense to me. So, come on now. Tell me out the truth. How do you really make your living?'

The artist looked suddenly old, defeated. The thoughts running through his mind could be all too easily read in his face: 'What kind of a land is this? Who is this massive dolt? How can he think he is the protector of anything? Will he turn violent and maybe strangle me?'

'Well?' said Fionn. 'I'm waiting.'

The artist looked around nervously, then saw what he had been hoping for – a stream flowing nearby.

'Come here. I will explain,' and he beckoned Fionn towards its bank. It took him a little while to find what he wanted, but when he did he knelt and called Fionn to him.

'There. Lean forward and tell me what you see.'

Fionn was alert now, suspecting some trick, for the water before them was deep and as still as death.

'Come. Come! Are you afraid of water, too? Tell me what do you see, eh?' Fionn cautiously leaned out, then pulled back, crossly.

'Sure, don't I know well what I'll see there. Myself.'

'Aha!' cried the man, and gave a little clap, which to Fionn sounded very much like more mockery. He got up.

'Hi! I told you once before that if you're trying to be funny with me it'd be very dangerous for you.'

'No, no, no! Try to forget all that. Now listen. What is seen on the water is a picture, the same as I make in my working. But I make it with paint instead of water. Now, do you understand?'

'Indeed I do not. Why would anyone want a picture of himself? Isn't it bad enough for a man to have his own self to put up with, never mind a thing that only looks like him? I'm suspicious of you, so I am. You're up to no good, I'm thinking, even though I don't like to say it of any man.'

The artist sighed wearily.

'What use is it to speak to this fathead?' he thought. But he said nothing.

It was Fionn who continued. 'Look, I think 'twould be better if you were coming along with me now. I have a few people I want you to meet, an' one man in particular.'

'The king himself, maybe?'

'We'll see about that, too. But I have someone else in mind, an' that's our chief of druids at Tara, Taoscán Mac Liath. If pictures an' painting are known about, he's the man that'll have the knowledge. So come on, an' we'll sort this out once an' for all.'

'Exactly as I wish to do,' beamed the artist. 'It is a pleasure I have long looked forward to, I assure you.'

And so they walked, Fionn glancing sideways occasionally at this odd person, trying to sort out in his mind all the various new ideas he had come upon today. But there was something else, too; something faintly suspicious, but which yet he could put no name on.

Long before they reached Tara the road began to become crowded. From a trickle of people and animals the traffic grew steadily until by the time they were in sight of the hill they were having to elbow their way through the crush – petitioners, servants, hucksters, beggars and occasional soldiers trying to clear a way for impatient and fuming charioteers. Fionn was accustomed to all this; it hardly cost him a second thought. But his companion began to show signs of nervousness as the jostling mob pushed him this way and that. He was holding his pack in his arms now, carefully to him, trying to protect it against injury. But it was doubtful whether he would reach the gate in safety. He cried out to Fionn, who was several steps ahead now, and luckily he heard him above the babble of voices. He glanced back, saw the artist sinking, then did the only thing possible: let an almighty roar out of him.

There was a sudden hush, a gaping of mouths in awe and fright. Even the struggling horses stopped, amazed.

'Is there any law or order in this cursed place at all once I go away for a while?' he bellowed. 'Well, I'm here again, so push back, or by Crom, I'll send the whole crowd of ye packing! Come on! Move.'

Between bodies shrinking back, faces scowling, voices muttering and croaking, there was a weird, even ridiculous little interval, Fionn towering severely over all, his hands on his hips. Then from the direction of the gate there came a flurry of feet, a clatter of weapons, and Diarmaid, Conán, Liagán and several other of the Fianna were on the spot.

'What's happening here?' demanded Diarmaid. 'Who's making all the noise? Have ye any regard for King Cormac's rest?'

Then he saw Fionn.

'Wisha, look who's back. An' how did things go below in Lár na hÉireann?' He advanced, all smiles. Fionn turned sourly and glared at him.

'Never mind about that. What's the meaning of this rabblement here? Didn't I give strict orders that no one was to come nearer than ten paces to the gate? Where's the line I marked in the ground here? Well?'

Diarmaid's smile looked frozen and foolish as he stood, unable to answer. Fionn looked at each of them in turn.

'Have this crowd moved well out from here before I get back. An' clear a way down to Taoscán's cave. I'll be wanting to talk to him soon.'

He beckoned the artist towards him and strode on into the courtyard while outside could be heard the scattering of the mob in a hail of fists, hobnails and curses.

'We'll go an' see himself first,' growled Fionn as they crossed towards an important-looking door which was severely guarded by two enormous fighting-men. They stepped nimbly aside as Fionn approached, knocked and entered almost all in the one movement. The artist was left alone under their fierce stare for a few moments, wondering what was next to come. Then Fionn emerged again, beckoned, and they entered a hushed hallway, a world away from the noise and dust outside. Here all was cool and dim. Servants moved hither and thither soundlessly; whispered conversations fluttered about them as they paced towards a second door. The single guard standing there, without so much as moving a muscle, hissed out of the corner of his mouth: 'Mind yourself. He's in a dirty mood today.'

Fionn nodded, the door was opened, and there before them, hands behind his back, staring out the window, stood King Cormac. He did not turn to look at them as they entered. He never once moved, even when Fionn cleared his throat and muttered an apology for disturbing him.

'I wouldn't dream of breaking in on you like this, only that I have someone here you might like to meet ... maybe.'

He was beginning to be doubtful now – for Cormac did not stir. But he spoke. And both men, for their different reasons, listened carefully, Fionn because he knew this man, the artist because he did not.

'What bellowing had you out there beyond at the gate? Didn't you know I amn't well at this time of the day?'

Then, as Fionn was about to make a well-rehearsed excuse, he continued without stopping: 'An' how is my forest? Is it still there, or have them cursed O'Carrolls the whole thing ruined?'

He wheeled about now, faced them, searbhas in his voice. 'That crowd'll have to be got rid of. That's all about it. 'Tis either them or my trees, an' don't be in any doubt which is the more important. But who's this you brought back with you? Is he one of 'em? How many trees did he make off with? If 'twas more than two we'll execute him now. This very minute!'

A short pause.

'It might cheer me up a bit, too,' he added solemnly as he turned back to the window and his staring.

'No, your highness.' Fionn tried hard to sound soothing. 'He's not one of the tree-stealers, but you're right when you said he might brighten up the day for you. He's a man that has many strange secrets. An' he's willing to share 'em with no one only yourself. Isn't that right, artist?'

18

He glowered fiercely at the man, his face silently threatening him to say 'yes'. What he said was far from what Fionn wanted to hear.

'My secrets would not be secrets if they were shared. That I will not do.'

Cormac never moved, only continued his staring. When he spoke at last his words were to the window, but Fionn knew they were meant for him and him only.

'So this is your way of brightening my day, is it?'

He whipped round then and glared at them both in quick succession.

'I have enough rebellious subjects already. What do I need one more for? Take him out of this an' throw him off of the back wall. Or better again, drown him below in the Boyne.'

The reaction could have been worse, Fionn thought. Better to say something sensible quick, though, while there was still hope.

'Your majesty, this lad here, he's from the wild an' dark land of Germany, an' he's in Ireland to learn whatever we can teach him about gentle living an' ...'

'Lies! What you say is not true!' interrupted the artist. 'It is the other way around. You must not say such things.'

He was obviously displeased. But Fionn was delighted. This was the way. Encourage the fellow to explain himself whether he liked it ot not.

'Wolves an' trolls is all that's in it. An' wild people, of course. That's what I heard, an' the man that told it to me was never known to tell a lie.'

The artist turned to Cormac, white in the face, shaking.

'Please, you must not believe him. I am a man, yes, with secrets. Some of them I will share with you' – and

19

he bowed – 'but others must not be spoken. Ever.'

Cormac eyed him.

'Look,' Cormac scowled, 'I'm not in the habit of having things I want kept from me. Take your choice. Tell me all, or you're for the river.'

The artist's face changed again. A look of disappointment and anger spread over it.

'These are not just words you speak, King Cormac. And it may be as you promise. But I would talk with your druid first.'

Cormac eyed him again, dangerously, then flicked his hand, waving him away like a piece of dirt.

'You can talk to Taoscán if you like ... but only after you talk to me first.'

Fionn saw that things were going from bad to worse, coughed and excused himself. His going was hardly noticed in that tense room. Outside the door he pulled the guard to him and whispered urgently: 'Breasal, listen! Get Taoscán. Now! Run!'

He licked his lips, re-entered the room, and found them in the same stance, Cormac still threatening, the artist defiant.

Quick! Play for time, he told himself. And hope that Taoscán is at home. He clapped, then rubbed his hands briskly to break the tension. He stepped in.

'Well, well. Ye're still here, are ye? I thought ye'd be having a great oul' chat by now, interesting men like ye.'

He smiled, hoping that it would improve matters. But when Cormac turned to him he knew that he had failed. And dismally, too.

'Fionn, you're gone too far this time. Trying to torment me you are. Well, d'you know what's going to happen to you – an' to this idiot you brought in here to annoy me?'

'I do not,' replied Fionn innocently. Better let him talk on, anyway, and hope that Taoscán would make no delay.

Cormac began a bloody litany of the torments he would surely see applied to every part of them, and the more gruesome the list became the more Fionn smiled.

'Good man. Keep it up,' he thought. 'But please, Taoscán, come soon.'

His smile seemed to urge Cormac on to ever greater threats, but at last even he ran out of torments. He paused for breath and in that lull a hurried shuffling was heard in the passage outside.

'Thanks be to Lugh,' murmured Fionn, 'Taoscán at last.'

It was none other. His voice entered before him.

'What's the trouble this time? No day I try to do a bit of work but I'm disturbed. Where are they, at all?'

And then he was in the room between them, his back stooped, grey beard and hair seeming to bristle as he looked from one to the other. His eyes were piercing, unafraid.

Fionn it was who slipped around to shut the door. Better that whatever might be said be kept private. For Taoscán had a way of addressing Cormac like a school-boy sometimes. No sense in letting the world know of that. It would do the royal image little good if it were told abroad.

But Taoscán spoke quietly and accused no one of anything yet.

'Why don't ye sit down while ye're standing, men? Useful thoughts are always best sat on.'

Fionn smiled. Trust Taoscán to take the sting out of the meeting.

When they were seated Taoscán turned to the artist

shrewdly. 'You're like a man that might be from Germany, I'd say. Am I right or wrong?'

Taoscán never ceased to amaze Fionn. How in the name of Macnamh could he have known such a thing!

'You are right. And soon I will be back there. Ireland is not a fit place for an artist such as I. That much I have found out this day.'

There might have been another flare-up, for Cormac snorted and half rose. But Taoscán restrained him with a gentle motion of his left hand and answered – 'A man can sometimes be mistaken. Not every day is the right one for visiting new places, new people. Look, Cormac, Fionn, would it please ye to let us talk together in private for a time? I have questions to put to him. An' I'm sure he has many things he'd like to hear an answer to, too.'

And he shepherded them out, with a final word to Fionn – 'I'll be down to the hall after a while. Wait for me there.'

An hour passed. Two hours. Still no sign of Taoscán.

'Begor, they must be having a great oul' conference, whatever 'tis all about. Let 'em at it. Men of learning like 'em could talk the leg off of an ass an' be nothing the worse for it.'

Supper-time came, but still no message. Fionn began to grow edgy.

'D'you think,' he said to Diarmaid, 'I should maybe go down an' have a look? Could that cursed fellow be after throttling Taoscán, or something? I never liked the look of him from the first time I laid eyes on him.'

They hummed and hawed, one man advising this, another that, until in the end no one did anything.

'Here!' cried Cormac at last, exasperated. 'The supper'll be destroyed on us. I'm going to eat, whatever about ye.'

They joined him gladly enough. Anything was better than waiting for something to happen. But the first joint had no more than been carved when the door opened and Taoscán sailed in, a sort of smile decorating his face. Every man stopped what he was at, expecting to see the artist too. But Taoscán was alone. Eyes glanced nervously back and forth as the Fianna tried to guess at what might have happened him.

Taoscán was well aware of their doubts, for he laughed as he took his usual place at the top table, pausing only to say, 'eat first, an' afterwards ye'll hear my news.'

They had to be content with that. Even Cormac could get no more out of him. It was one of the shortest suppers that year in Tara. Food was wolfed down, eaten as if it were only so much hay, to be got through and done with in expectation of something better. And when all was hushed again and the crockery cleared away, Taoscán leaned forward on his elbows and began quietly.

'We have talked long an' hard, this man and me. I find that he has strange thoughts in his head. Some of them I am not pleased with, but if any man here asked me why, I could not tell him. But I do know that there is mystery there, and something dark.'

'Hold on a minute,' said Cormac, tapping his fingers on the table. 'Where is he, before you go any farther?'

'Asleep. He begged to be excused. He has walked so far these last few days that he feared he would seem rude if he fell asleep in your presence.'

'Awake or asleep, he was rude anyway. Even worse, he was insolent. An' I don't like people who don't know their place.'

'Your choice it is, Cormac. He can be allowed to stay, or be put out now.'

23

'Well ... tell us what else ye said first. No sense in disturbing ourselves now.'

Taoscán nodded. 'If there are certain things about this man I do not like, there are others that appeal to me.'

'Tell us,' said Fionn, rubbing his hands, excited at the prospect of a story.

'Well, he has shown me the contents of his bag.'

'The very thing I forgot to tell ye,' yelped Fionn. 'Is it all the little crocks with the colours on 'em?'

'Those also. But there was more.'

'The little flat packet?'

'Yes.'

'Didn't I clean forget to ask him what was in it. Did he open it for you?'

'Yes,' and Taoscán hesitated, looked long at his fingers. 'But only after much persuading and some threats.'

He seemed reluctant to talk more about it.

'Come on,' urged Cormac. 'Don't be keeping us in the horror of suspense. What was in it?'

'A picture.'

The very word was strange to them. It was muttered and passed from mouth to mouth around the tables for some time. No one wished to appear stupid by asking what a picture was, but at last Diarmaid could stand it no longer.

'Tell us more,' he pleaded. 'An' make it exciting if you can.'

Taoscán almost smiled. 'I'll tell you what happened, so, Diarmaid. No more, no less.'

They settled to listen.

'This picture, it was of a man's head. A face. An' the minute I saw it, I thought, "I know who he is, even if I can't put a name on him at the moment". I said that to him too, but no! It couldn't be so, he said. The man was

24

his beloved teacher, the one who had taught him the skills of making wondrous colours into pictures. How could I, from Ireland in the far west, have met such a man, who lived in the darkest forest of Thuringia and had taken seven pupils only in all his years there? It was impossible.'

'But why would a man like that, who's so good at his business, want to be wasting his time in a forest – a dark one, too – when he could be at the court of the emperor of the world?' put in Cormac, curiously.

'The very thing that was troubling myself,' answered Taoscán. 'But the only answer I could get was that this great artist was at work, preparing the "Picture of the World", as he called it. And for that he needed quietness. That was why he took only one helper, at any time, so that he would be helped without being disturbed.'

'Disturbed in the mind he must be, surely,' mused Oisín.

'That may be so, indeed,' murmured Taoscán. 'But what was annoying me was that the more I looked at the face the more certain I was that, yes, I had met that man somewhere.'

'A good or bad meeting?' asked Fionn.

'I couldn't be certain, but I think I'd remember if something good had come out of it. But more than that I couldn't say.'

'Well, tell us the rest, anyway, an' you can be thinking about that some other time.'

'The rest is simple enough. He has two jars along with the jars of colours, an' no matter what way I asked him he would not open 'em for me. They were his special secret, he said, what he had learned in his seven years in the forest, an' if the jars were opened everything he had worked so hard for would be ruined.'

'What oul' nonsense is that?' cried Cormac, sitting up. 'He's up to no good if he has secrets inside in jars. How do we know it isn't poison that's in 'em, an' that he won't kill the whole lot of us in our sleep?'

'True,' nodded Taoscán. 'But I can understand what he says. Knowledge is a thing not found growing on the trees. Sometimes it is hard earned. Look at my shelves below. Or at my books. I have things there – spells, cures, even curses – that cannot be told, some from my grandmother, others from here,' – tapping his forehead. 'No tortures or promises could make me reveal them. So maybe he has things the like of those in his two jars.'

They could not deny the truth of what he said.

'Anything else?' said Fionn hopefully, though it seemed now that there would be no story after all, since there were more questions than answers.

Taoscán brightened.

'Yes. He said to tell you, King Cormac, that he would be honoured to paint for you a picture on any wall in Tara.'

'Hah? I wouldn't let him touch one of 'em. How do I know but he'd put a spell on it? The whole place could fall down around our ears.'

But after a moment he looked again at Taoscán.

'What sort of picture had he in his mind?'

'Anything you wanted, he'd do it. That's what he said. He was afraid he had displeased you above in the room, so he wants to make it up to you.'

'Hmmm! Well, maybe I'll give him a chance, so.'

It was clear that Cormac was pleased that the fellow had come to his senses, no doubt under the good influence of Taoscán's wisdom.

'All right. I'll think about it. We'll see him in the morning, when I rise.'

The feasters broke up soon after and every man went to his own bed wondering what new things the morning might bring.

They were soon enough to be pleasantly surprised.

EXACTLY ONE HOUR AFTER CORMAC had bathed and breakfasted the following day the artist was ushered into his presence. Taoscán and Fionn were present, as well as several others of the Fianna, all anxious to see what would come of the meeting. Cormac came straight to the point.

'Well, now! I'm told you're going to do a picture for us. Am I right or wrong?'

'You are right, your highness. And a picture that will delight your heart.'

'I'm glad to hear you saying it. Now, what'll be in this picture?'

'Anything you demand I will paint.'

Now that he had a choice Cormac was lost for words. He leaned aside to Taoscán.

'Tell me, what am I going to ask for?'

'Something bright an' happy. Tell him to make the darkest room in the house into a summer's day. If he can do that much, he knows his trade.'

Cormac smiled. A crafty look was in his eye when he turned to the artist, then to Fionn.

'Take him down, Fionn, an' show him the Black Hole. If he can brighten that place I might even give him the job of painting the rest of the palace – an' pay him for it.'

Taoscán seemed not so amused by this and he said as much when Fionn and the artist had gone out.

'Cormac, you have badness in your mind for him yet. Why can't you take him at his word. Maybe he is trying to be friendly.'

'I still don't trust him. But I'll be fair as fair can be. If

he can do a job on the place below I'll give him a welcome.'

'An' if it fails him?'

'Heh! He can live with it, 'cos 'tis there he'll stay for
a year an' a day, inside in the same Black Hole.'

This reply sounded to Taoscán very much like one of
Cormac's bad attempts at verse. He shook his head. It
was not mannerly or hospitable, this type of act, and well
he knew it. But he would not argue yet. Better to wait
and see what might happen.

Even Fionn felt a twinge of sympathy for the stranger
as he jammed the torch into an iron bracket and unbarred
the heavy iron-studded door of dungeon Number Seven,
the deepest in Tara. Well it had been named the Black
Hole, for it was forty-two steps under the level of the
nearest floor above and never a splink of nature's light
entered it. None but the most hardened villains were
ever lodged there, and for short spells only, for it had the
reputation of driving men out of their wits. And the
proof of it was all around – long nail-scrapes in the solid
stone, tooth marks on the metal of the door, and a shiny
track worn into the floor from corner to corner. Many a
hardy man had walked his final hours away, cackling
foolishly in that terrible darkness with no one to heed his
cries, no mother's love to help him into the next world.

By the light of the torch the artist examined it. If he
felt afraid or disgusted, he showed none of it, only turned, thanked Fionn and said: 'It is a challenge to me, this
place. But I will prove to you that I do as I say.'

He looked at the ugly walls confidently. 'Soon men
will come, they will beg to be locked into this room. And
those in it, they will be dragged out only by force.'

Fionn sniggered. He did not wish to show disrespect,
but the thought of the Black Hole being a desired place

was amusing in a sort of way. Or was it fear that made the man speak so? Fionn peered at him. He certainly appeared as normal as ever, bustling about, measuring with hand and eye, humming a little tune. Then he placed his pack in the centre of the floor, stood and said to Fionn in a voice which rang with authority, 'thank you. Now go, please. I must begin. Alone.'

'But what about light? That torch'll burn out in half an hour or less.'

'I will call if I need a thing. Let a servant be placed at the door above. But now I must work. So go! Go!'

He said no more, only stood watching until Fionn had gone out shrugging and feeling his way along the short corridor to the steps. Then he carefully undid the pack, placed the stone pots in a circle around him, unwrapped the picture and stared hard at it, muttering as he did so. He did not unpack the two special jars.

When Fionn returned to the others he was thoughtful. 'Why would anyone want to be down in a place like that on his own?' he said, to no one in particular.

'Tell us, what happened?' They were all ears as he described what he had seen and heard. Even Taoscán was surprised.

'There's something wrong somewhere. I can't put my finger on it, but there's a buzzing in my head, an' that's a warning of danger.'

'There *will* be danger – for him, if he can't do what he said,' leered Cormac. 'I'm looking forward to seeing the end of this, whatever about the rest of ye.'

''Tis that very part of it I'm not so sure about,' said Taoscán more soberly, but few ears were listening. Men were chattering now about the man below, wondering what might he do that could make men clamour to be put into such a place. No doubt about it, it was a thing worth waiting for!

And wait they did. For all of two impatient days and nights. Yet, during that time the servant was not once called to bring food, drink or light. Nothing.

'Could he be dead, Fionn, d'you think?' said Cormac. Even he was worried, afraid of being cheated of a great wonder.

'I don't rightly know. But if he isn't out of it by dawn tomorrow I'll go down.'

'Make sure to set the cock for early,' Cormac ordered his chamber-attendant last thing before his head hit the pillow that night. He was excited, though he would not have admitted it.

They were all up at first light – woken by the same royal cock's raucous cackling. But still no sound from below. And the servant at the door had nothing to report.

'I'll have to go in there myself,' declared Fionn. ''Tis the only way.'

He approached the iron-bound door carefully, torch flaming in his hand ... only to be greeted by heavy snoring! He stopped, startled. He listened. There it was, without a doubt, the steady rasping of a man deep in contented sleep.

'Well, could you credit that,' Fionn muttered, still unsure of himself. 'The lazy animal is sleeping. Begor, if that job isn't done there'll be more noise down here than that.' He pounced on the door, threw off the iron bar and stepped into ... But into what? The place that had been a lonesome dungeon was now ablaze with colour. A bright sun shone from a clear, blue sky. Birds stretched from trees, seeming to eye him laughingly. Grass, flowers – and what gorgeous flowers – leaves, cattle; they were all here. And lying in a comfortable grassy hollow was the artist, his hands behind his head, smiling up at Fionn.

'I was hoping it was yourself that would come,' was his first greeting.

Fionn could only stand gaping, awestruck. What place was this? How could the sun, flowers, cows ... ? His thoughts trailed off as his eyes tried to take it in. No words came to him. He shook his head even as his lips moved soundlessly.

'Magic,' he croaked. "Tis magic, nothing else.'

'No magic,' smiled the artist, rising. 'All you see before you was done by this.'

He held out his left hand. Fionn drew back.

'Keep out from me! Don't touch me. I can't ...'

Words failed him again, and he stumbled back into the corridor, conscious only now, suddenly, of the torch still burning in his hand. He looked at it stupidly.

'I'm in a dream. I have to be. But by Crom, if I am I'll soon know if everyone else is too.'

He ran for the stairs, hardly hearing the laughter of the artist welling up after him out of the darkness below. When he flung himself into the group clustered about the door above he looked half-crazed, so much so that men snatched at their swords, expecting some terrible thing to be on his heels.

When nothing appeared they looked again. At him. At the door. They were confused. Taoscán pressed forward.

'What is it, Fionn? You look like you saw a ghost. What's down there, in ainm Lugh?'

'I'm not sure now whether I saw it or not,' he mumbled. 'But tell me this. Could I be going mad? Do I look astray?'

They glanced at each other.

'How so? What d'you mean?'

'Mad! Not correct in the head. That's what I mean.

'Cos I'm after seeing the sun shining down there in the Black Hole. An' cows in the fields.'

A pause, while they tried to come to terms with this.

'Fields, Fionn? Down where?' asked Taoscán gently.

'Amn't I telling you! Below in the Hole.'

Taoscán sighed but did not pursue the matter. Instead he asked, 'Is that fellow still down there?'

Fionn nodded.

'Well, that's something, at least. I'll go down an' have a word with him.'

'Do,' said Fionn. 'An' be sure to tell me if I'm gone mad when you come back.'

Taoscán went below, led nervously by Diarmaid holding a torch in one had, his sword in the other.

Moments later they were back, out of breath, mouths twitching, confusion on their faces.

'Well?' demanded Fionn. 'Did ye see it? Did ye? Or was it my eyes playing up on me?'

'No, indeed, Fionn,' replied Taoscán in a serious, quiet voice. 'You saw what you saw, an' so did we.'

'Will ye stop talking in riddles,' spluttered Cormac, 'an' tell the rest of us straight out what's down there.'

'Better you see it for yourself, highness, 'cos there's no words invented yet that could describe it to you.'

'Begor, it must be some marvel entirely,' and he stepped cautiously down to investigate for himself, two guards before him, two more behind.

The dazed look on his face when he returned frightened not a few of those standing by. Conán made to assist him but was waved feebly away, while Fionn even managed a whiskery smile. At least his sanity was not in question now, he knew.

Word spread like the wind after that to the four corners of the land ... 'the magic room is found' ... 'Cormac, the cute sleeveen, was keeping it all for himself' ... 'the like of it ... never before seen' ... and as the rumours widened out the story grew until all the previous wonders of the earth were as nothing by comparison in men's minds. A huge queue began to form outside the gates of Tara and soon those within were besieged and almost deafened by shouts of, 'We want to see the magic room. Let us in or we'll break down the gates'.

They would have, too, had not Taoscán thought of a plan to control events.

'Everyone that wants to see it must pay a fee,' he declared, and men had to be content with that, for if they grumbled or hesitated there were a hundred others to take their place in the line.

And so the money began to pour into Cormac's treasure chests.

''Tis a thing I never thought I'd see under the sky of Ireland,' he laughed, clapping Taoscán on the back, 'that men would pay a tax with a smile on their faces. Don't it prove, too, that there be miracles in the world?'

Taoscán said nothing, merely frowned.

A day came at last, however, when all the chests that the royal carpenters and blacksmiths could make were full, and the clink of money began to get on even Cormac's nerves.

'What'll I do with all of it? We'll have to start a war or something to try to get rid of some of it.'

Easier said than done, for even his enemies had laid down their arms and were queuing at the gate, fee in hand. In any case, Taoscán would have none of that kind of politics. Added to that, the constant noise of people arguing, singing, bickering, fighting, complaining day and night began to have its effect. Sleep became a thing of the past in Tara; even the men of the Fianna could take no more. They came to Fionn in a huddle with Diarmaid as their spokesman.

'Look, we might as well be in Gleann na nGealt as here.'

Fionn looked at him from haggard eyes.

'We'd be a lot better off there. At least mad people often find their wits in that place. Here you'd lose any you ever had.'

'But what are we going to do about it? If this lasts much longer there'll be a mutiny.'

'I'll see Taoscán. He'll know what to do, if anyone can.'

And again Taoscán came to the rescue. He said to Cormac: 'Look, while that place below has the only such painting in the land we'll have crowds wanting to gape at it. But 'tis too small. That's what has us ruined. 'Tis taking all day for a few people to get in to see it. My advice now is to get him to paint every wall in the place. That way, it won't be a mystery any more an' they'll soon stop coming.'

Cormac was not convinced. 'Wouldn't it be a lot easier to lock it up, or scrape the walls? Or even fill the place up with water?'

'D'you think men'd accept that? People only believe what they want to, an' they'd say again you were trying to keep it all to yourself. No, there could be rebellion in the land if you do that.'

And so it was that Taoscán once more got his way. The artist was persuaded to go to work, given free rein as to where or when he wanted to paint. The only instruction that Cormac gave him, in fact, was: 'Don't forget to put in a few big battles, something to keep us reminded of the good oul' days when I was younger an' fighting fit.'

34

Oddly, the artist was in no way reluctant to oblige.

'If you will describe them, I will do the rest, your gracious highness. Once I have a story in my head I never forget it.'

It pleased Cormac to do that, and he had help aplenty from the Fianna in jogging his memory, for they were nothing if not proud of the great splittings and maimings to men and scatterings of mighty armies they had accomplished down the years. By night the battles were unfolded in story, and by day the artist fixed them to the walls in all their gory detail, scene after scene.

Cormac and a few others were permitted to see each day's finished work, but the artist would allow no one to be present while he painted. Taoscán seemed set to protest at this, then thought better of it and merely stroked his beard. Something still bothered him, but whatever it was, he kept it to himself. The only complaint the men had was that while the feasting-hall was being painted they had to eat in the yard – when the weather permitted.

But at last it was completed, and they crowded in to see for themselves if their wait had been worthwhile. What greeted them put the Black Hole in the shade, if that were possible. Chariots, flashing swords, men twisted, falling, horses plunging; all were there, as alive, it seemed, as if the past had risen again and all those dead heroes had come to life. Round and round surged the battle, from one wall to the next, in an unending frenzy. And those looking at it could only stare, mesmerised, for what was on the walls seemed even more real than themselves. They each nodded appreciation, muttered what few words they could still command in congratulation, and shambled away to think about it, alone.

Again the word spread and once more Tara was

besieged, only this time things were managed better. The visitors were moved on ever faster, even more money rolled in and everyone seemed to get happier by the day. In the midst of all this the artist worked on, room by room, until he had been at Tara almost twelve months.

Then, on an evening in the fading season of that year, an alarming thing happened. The second-last room at the top end of the palace was being painted and Fergus – whom the men had nicknamed 'Fiosrach' because of his curiosity – and Dioraing, one of the other guards on sentry-duty that night, were passing the door of that same chamber when they noticed that it was open. Fergus, as was so natural for him, poked in his head, saw that there was no one inside, and decided – in the interests of security, of course – to have a peep.

'What harm can it do?' he said to his companion. 'Isn't Cormac an' Taoscán nearly gone blind from having the first look at all the fine pictures. Time we had our turn, too.'

They crept in and looked admiringly at the work already completed. It was yet another battle-scene, crammed with men, dogs and horses. But Fergus, whatever way he looked at it, found it not entirely to his satisfaction, and said so.

'There's something missing,' he declared flatly.

'Missing?' said Dioraing. 'What could be missing from a scene the like of that? Isn't it a finished piece of work entirely.'

'It isn't, then. There's a thing – an' I can't say rightly what it is yet – not correct about it.'

Fergus had always had the reputation of being a hard man to please. He had no intention of losing it now.

'Look, whatever it might be, come on out of here, before he comes back an' finds us. You know he doesn't like anyone to see what he's doing until 'tis all finished.'

They left, though Fergus was determined to return. But first he went and by lamplight looked again at all the other battle-scenes, detail by little detail. Yet the same unnamed thing continued to worry him. The following day he was still examining them, and no one thought that at all odd; after all, he was the curious one. But what was this sudden interest in the pictures that had him squinting at them all hours of the day and from all angles? No one could answer that. And then it came to him, suddenly and without warning, the answer. He clicked his fingers and yelled with delight: 'That's it! I knew there was something missing.'

Fionn questioned him, fearing he was ill.

'What's wrong with you, Fergus? If 'tis so you have anything missing in your head go down to Taoscán. He'll put it right.'

Fergus merely smiled, winked at Fionn, and walked away obviously bouncing with excitement.

'A strange man always,' muttered Fionn. ''Tis all right if he isn't going dark in the mind this time, though. I'll have to keep an eye to him.'

If he had done so they might have been spared what was about to happen.

FERGUS HURRIED BACK TO the room where the artist was now at work again, pushed in the door before him and announced: 'I found the fault! I know what 'tis.'

The artist jerked with fright, leaving a long smudge across the figures he had been working on. In a rage he turned.

'Who dares to enter? You will suffer torments for this!'

There was poison in the way he said it. Fergus

stopped in mid-step, and seeing the look of hatred in the face staring at him, his courage began to falter.

'I'm ... I'm sorry, a dhuine. I didn't ... I only meant to tell you that I ... found out what it was that's wrong ...' and he darted a nod towards the painting.

'Wrong?' said the artist icily. 'Wrong? It is you who are wrong. In your mind.'

'The very thing that Fionn said.' Fergus tried to laugh, hoping that he sounded convincing. In an instant, at the mention of Fionn's name, the artist's expression changed. Even his voice was milder when he spoke again, almost wheedling.

'But I always wish to listen,' he said. 'Perhaps there *is* something you have to say that I should hear. Maybe even I can make a mistake. Tell me, then, what it is.'

Fergus' hands were sweaty, and shaking, but with relief now. After that first outburst he had hardly dared to hope he might bring himself out of the room without injury or worse. So he was quick to take his chance now.

''Tis like this, noble person. I was noticing that in all the paintings on all the walls – this one here as well as the rest – you have a lot of people.'

The artist never even blinked as he replied, 'in battles there must be people. What of it?'

'But with all those people there isn't a face to be seen. Why is that?'

The man stared long and hard at Fergus, as if memorising every detail of his countenance. But he did not answer the question, only turned away, padded across the room and stood by the door, considering. When he spoke it was in a whisper.

'Well you have observed, my friend. And your question must be answered. But not now.'

He recrossed the room and stopped suddenly. 'Can

you keep a secret for a short time? For one day?'

'I s'pose I can ... Depending on what 'tis, of course.'

'That you will know soon enough. Before this time tomorrow all will be revealed to you, and only you. Can you be content with that?'

'Well, I'm curious to know, but if I'll find out tomorrow I'll wait. Sure, what difference will a day make?'

'What difference, indeed?' said he smoothly. But if Fergus had taken note of the dark gleam in his eye then he might have had second thoughts on the matter.

As it was, he spent the rest of the day in a fritter of impatience, wishing the time gone that stood between him and the answer to his question. In bed that night he was the same, tossing and turning, unable to sleep long after all his companions were in the land of dreams. It was some time in the small hours when his eyes finally closed. How was he to know that they would never re-open to this world?

A few moments later, a heavy paw was jammed to his throat, another over his face. He tried to struggle, to cry out, but all was over in seconds. His neck was crushed and snapped like a twig and even before his legs and hands had stopped twitching, ten dagger-sharp black claws had sunk into the flesh below his ears. Slowly, horribly the skin burst and tore as Fergus' face was wrenched in one piece off the bones of his skull.

WHEN FIONN GOT NO reply to his second knock the following morning, he became angry.

'Fergus is getting lazy as well as odd. I'll give him an extra job or two today, bedad – as soon as I rout him out of the bed.'

He thrust in the door and strode to where Fergus was lying.

'Out of it, you lazy reptile! Come on, jump!'

No move.

Fionn prodded the sheepskin rugs with his toe.

'One last time I'll tell you an' that's all. Get out of it this instant, or else!'

This kind of thing could not be tolerated. An inspection-parade in a few minutes' time by the king himself, and this fellow still in bed! Cormac would accuse Fionn of becoming slack.

'That's it, so,' he shouted when there was still no move, and he flung the rugs aside.

The sight of the bare bones leering up at him gave Fionn such a jolt that he froze, hardly noticing the dark mess of blood-soaked straw and clothing. He was no coward – far from it – and had seen all types of battle-injuries and weapon-wounds in his time, but this was different. Never had he come across the like of it before. Who or what would tear the face off a man and leave the rest of him untouched?

'But wait,' he told himself as he tried to control the nausea that rose in his throat. 'Wait! There *was* one like it.' And as it came back to him the little hairs at the back of his neck began to stand on end. 'The Conriocht of Gleann Garbh used to do this kind of thing too. But, sure, didn't we kill him a long time ago. Or at least I was sure we did,' he whispered nervously, glancing again at what had been Fergus. 'Better to get Taoscán. If any man can settle this, he can.'

Hardly had he raised the alarm than Taoscán Mac-Liath was on the scene, all the others crushing in behind him, anxious to see. He did not try to stop them, but when they had looked their fill – but touched nothing on his express orders – he cleared everyone, including Fionn and the artist, out of the room. The latter had come with

40

the rest and expressed his disgust just as they did.

'An unnatural deed, surely. Only a wild animal could do it.'

'Hmmm!' was Taoscán's only reply as he closed the door behind him and went to work.

It was not a pleasant job he had to do, but his old nerves were still as strong as his head was clear. The Fianna, in the meantime, were not so calm. Shock soon turned to anger and that to fear.

'Dar fia, but wasn't it a low class of a deed.'

'Low? Whatever did it should be cut up into four pieces an' hung out in the wind to swing.'

'If the savage can be found, that is. Isn't it strange that he woke none of us while he was doing the dirty act. Couldn't we all have been killed in our sleep as well as Fergus?'

'Maybe that's what'll happen tonight. None of us is safe.'

And so it went on, until Fionn ordered them to cease.

'Shut up, will ye! Ye're like a crowd of oul' cailleachs, trying to frighten each other. I can't even think while ye're gabbing.'

Not that there were too many thoughts crowding each other in his head just then. But rumours were evil things, and dangerous when men were frightened. Better to kill them off at once, before they spread their ugly roots.

WHEN TAOSCÁN CAME OUT at length, his job done, there was a dour look on his face.

'Your highness,' he said evenly, 'I have no choice but to tell you the truth, though it may not please your ears.'

'Well, do so, anyway.'

'Fergus' face was stolen.'

'Stolen?' Cormac, as well as everyone else, was uncomprehending. 'Stolen? But tell us, Taoscán, who'd steal a face? What good is a person's face to anyone?'

'That's what I don't know,' sighed the old man. 'But 'tis what I intend to find out,' and the way he looked each of them over as he said it made them squirm uncomfortably. Did he know more than he was prepared to say?

If that was the case it did not show, for though he gave it his full attention for the next three days there was no further development. Fergus was buried and they all went reluctantly – or relieved – back to their posts. And in the upper chamber the artist resumed his painting, this time keeping the door securely bolted.

A week passed. Then two. There were no new deaths and gradually men relaxed, even began to put the horrible deed a little to the back of their minds. All except Taoscán. Like a dog with a bone, he refused to let it go.

'I won't rest quiet until I find out what it was that killed him. Or where it went – or came from.'

Yet he did not find an answer.

A YEAR FLEW BY. The palace was long painted and the artist had even obliged some of the other lords of the land and decorated their homes too – all with Cormac's permission, of course. But nowhere else would he paint scenes of battle. These were reserved, he said, for Tara alone. Fionn he had made an exception for, however, but when he arrived at the Hill of Allen to examine the walls, Maighnis, Fionn's wife, would have none of it.

'You can paint all the flowers or trees you like, but no battles. I'm sick an' tired of hearing himself boasting about all that kind of oul' nonsense. Swords an' chariots, blood an' guts spilled out over this or that fine hill or

42

field is all he can talk about. You'd swear men had nothing better to be doing than maiming other poor mothers' sons.'

This talk of hers did not seem to please him much. He answered haughtily, 'men in combat there must be. Without them what use are flowers, trees? Those I will paint, or nothing.'

'If that's the way of it, do it somewhere else,' she snapped. And he left in a huff growling, his pack on his back.

Fionn was not amused when he found out.

'Now look what you did, you óinseach. You insulted him. When'll we ever get someone like that to come to us again?'

'Look at the big amadán that's calling me an óinseach! We're better off owing nothing to that lad. I didn't like the look of him, anyway.'

And she could not be moved from that strong opinion, though Fionn tried and tried again to make her reconsider.

When he returned to Tara early the following day he was surprised to find the Fianna going about their tasks and a bustling air of business over the whole place.

'What's all this?' he asked Diarmaid. 'Sure I'm not late, or anything? Why is everyone up an' working so early?'

'By Crom,' said Diarmaid, 'we were just going to send for you, but he said not to bother.'

'Who said?' Fionn was mystified.

'Who else but the painter? He said he was taking himself off home, that he had enough time spent here.'

'Did he look angry, by any chance?' Fionn was thinking of his wife's hard words.

'Not a bit of it. He was all smiles when the men were

lined up there in the yard to say goodbye to him.'

'The men ... lined up?'

'He asked that much as one last favour, an' I s'pose Cormac could hardly refuse him, after all the fine work he did here.'

'Tell me more.' Such a farewell parade had only ever been granted to royalty before now. It made him feel ... unwanted ... that it had been done without him.

'Well,' replied Diarmaid, 'there isn't a lot to tell. Conán filled in for you, an' everything went off as good as if you were here yourself.'

'Never mind that!' snapped Fionn. 'What did the lad say?'

'Devil a much. He said a few words about how proud he was to have brought pictures to Ireland, an' thanked everyone who had made him welcome, an' said he was sure he'd meet some of us again. Then he went along the ranks, nodded to each man and passed on.'

Diarmaid had finished and Fionn was turning away when he seemed to remember something else.

'Oh, yes, I forgot. There was just one thing I found a bit odd. It might be nothing, now, but I don't know why he'd do it.'

'Who? Do what?' Fionn halted, immediately interested.

'Well, he stopped in front of three men, like it'd be an honour or something, took each one of 'em by the hand, looked at him, but never said a word. I know that much for sure, 'cos I have it from Conán. An' he was walking behind him all the time.'

'What men were they? I want to talk to them.'

'One of 'em is your own shield-man, Sciabhrach. The others were Fearadach and Garad.'

Fionn paused, considering. What was special about

those three? Nothing immediately registered with him. He thanked Diarmaid, then strode off to meet with Cormac first. That had to be done to avoid giving insult. And maybe his highness would have more news to add.

He found, however, that Cormac was in no mood for talk. It even seemed to Fionn that he himself was being blamed for something, though no word to that effect was said. Obviously Cormac was unhappy that *his* artist was gone, but what, thought Fionn, had that to do with him? Why should he be blamed? He returned to the Hill of Allen that same day angry, determined to take Bran and Sceolaing on a hunt the next day, far away, alone, and to put all these recent events behind him.

He was up at cock-crow and off, westwards towards the great Bog of Allen before even Maighnis could question him. At the edge of that lonely, flat expanse he turned south-west to where Sliabh Bladhma, his earliest home, hunched on the horizon. There, among the haunts of his youth, he would think what thoughts he chose. At least he would be alone, away from all the prattle of stupid people, with no one but the dogs. And even when he realised, half-way home, that he had forgotten to interrogate the three men, he did not turn back. 'Time enough later,' he muttered. He hurried on, his troubles lightening with every step he put between his back and Tara.

'I must do this more often,' he told himself. 'I'm getting too caught up entirely in things that are no concern of mine.'

It was evening when he reached the lower slopes of the mountains and the soft wind in his hair brought a tear to his eye. Other days came flooding back to him, hunts, hours spent bathing in the icy hill-streams, and the taste of blackberries on warm autumn evenings. That and the memory of Bodhmhall, the old one who had

45

cared for him as though he were her own. Her cave was only a short distance from where he now stood. He paused in his mad scramble uphill. Should he revisit it? It was empty now; of that he felt sure. How many years had she been dead? Twenty-five? Thirty? Maybe the sight of it would be too painful, but how could he not visit it now that he was so close? Mind made up, he changed direction and bounded towards it, the dogs yapping and panting at either side.

He saw the familiar overhanging cliff long before the cave came into view and a wave of recognition surged through him, the same as he had felt that evening when he brought home his first-ever deer. How delicious the meat had tasted ... How pleased she had been, Bodh-mhall, praising him, laughing and encouraging.

And when the black mouth of the cave gaped before him, but forbidding rather than welcoming, he stopped, breathing heavily, staring. Again his old fears replaced the glad thoughts of moments before. It would be empty, bare, cold; that he knew. But yet something drew him. Curiosity, maybe? Or a ridiculous hoping against hope that it might still be as he remembered it? He hesitated. Should he enter?

It was the dogs that decided him. Bran was already dashing towards the darkness of the opening, Sceolaing just behind, as if all the game in the world were within for the taking. They vanished inside and Fionn was immediately back again in the present. He scrambled across, calling them as he leaped, and was at the cave before he realised it. The sudden gloom inside stopped him in his tracks and as his eyes darted here and there, taking in the almost-forgotten details of the place, the frenzied snuffling and chasing of the dogs went completely unnoticed by him.

The coldness of it shocked him. And the dark. Where had the light and laughter gone? The welcoming table? The fire just to the right of the entrance? But gone they were. All of them. The walls were bare and a damp clamminess hung in the very air. If a bear or a family of badgers had greeted him then it would have surprised him not in the least. The bleakness of it all staggered him.

He sat, silent, the dogs quiet also now, looking at him curiously. Fionn was not himself, and they knew it.

How long he remained there lost in his thoughts he did not know. He was brought to himself with a start by a noise in the distance. Low at first it sounded, then more distinctly until it rose up, still thin but majestic and urgent in the quiet of the gathering night. Immediately he recognised it. But even so he listened again, now intently. No. There could be no mistaking that for anything else. It was the Dord Fiann, that warning trumpet-blast of King Cormac's men, the most urgent call to arms and action. Danger it spelled. Mortal danger. It would not, must not, go unanswered, even for the briefest space of time, while any one of the Fianna remained alive to respond to its summons.

'Wouldn't you know it!' groaned Fionn. 'The very first chance I get to come here, I'm called out of it even before I can look around.'

But there was nothing for it only to collect himself and go, dislike it as he might.

He did not have to call the dogs. They too had heard the Dord and were already outside and scurrying off down into the darkening valley. Fionn had to check them once or twice, but it was as much a desire for their company as any wish to slow them that made him do it. There was a lonesomeness in the air and now, on top of that, came this urgent call. Something was wrong.

With a growing sense of gloom he hurried on through the darkness, his mind racing.

IN THE GREY LIGHT before dawn he reached the gates of Tara.

'Halt!' shouted a voice ahead, then another. 'Who is it? Name yourself!'

'Good,' he thought. 'At least the watch is alert. The danger can't be at its worst yet.'

Two sentries stepped warily towards him, spears at the ready. A torch flared. Delight and recognition.

'Fionn, is it yourself? Dar fia, but we're glad to see your face. Things are rightly upside down since you went, an' Cormac is tearing out bunches of his beard with worry. He'll be glad to see you, too.'

'His beard, eh? Well, it might be no harm to trim it a bit,' Fionn mused, but kept the opinion to himself. Better find out in person, as always, how things stood. He saluted the guards and passed in.

Diarmaid ran to meet him before he was halfway across the yard. He was in a state of near-panic.

'Fionn! By Crom, but you're the welcome sight. They're all inside in the hall there an' you'd swear every one of 'em was under some spell or other. They're staring out –'

'Hold on! Stop! Say no more.' He put his hands on Diarmaid's shoulders and shook him.

'Look,' he said urgently, 'come in here for a couple of minutes out of the light an' tell me, quick, what's happening.'

'Happening? Everything is happening. Three more good men gone to the land of the dead, an' never a chance to defend themselves.'

Fionn gritted his teeth. Somehow, he had expected

this or something like it.

'Who were they?'

'Sciabhrach, Garad an' Fearadach.'

'Did they get the same end as Fergus?'

'The very same. In the dark of the night,' and he glanced nervously into the furthest corners of the yard.

'I tell you, Fionn, there wasn't a wink of sleep got here since you went.'

Fionn was almost glad to hear it. Maybe that would teach Cormac to value his services more than he usually did.

'I s'pose I'd better be going in,' he sighed, nodding towards the hall.

'Be prepared for the worst. Himself is in no good humour, I can tell you.'

Fionn merely threw up his eyes and started in the direction of the door.

'Don't lose your temper, whatever else you do. Or we could all be ar slí na fírinne before too long.'

Good advice, thought Fionn as he climbed the three steps and knocked.

The scene that met him could have been from a normal quiet supper on any ordinary night. All except for one thing – and Fionn noticed it at once: there was not a sound from all the seated crowd. No music, no poetry, no talk. Not even the rattle of a knife on wood. It was downright eerie, and Fionn had to look again to assure himself that they were really alive. So he was almost relieved when Cormac, from the top table, let a bellow out of him which caused men to leap a foot out of their seats.

'You're back, are you? An' it isn't before time, either. We thought you were gone for good in the hour of danger. Where were you?'

Fionn was stung by this obvious insult but the look

of sheer relief in the faces of the men at his mere entry calmed him. And Taoscán's smile, as well as a little flick of his fingers, left him in no doubt that he was welcome. Even the scowl on the sulky fat face of Cairbre, the king's eldest son, could not dampen his sense of being where he belonged. And so he strode up the hall, took his place as usual, then called for meat, still not answering Cormac's question. Only when his cloak had been taken and he was settled comfortably, a goblet of mead in his hand, did he turn and slowly answer.

'Your majesty, I have been thinking on the recent strange events.'

'You don't know the half of 'em!' interrupted Cormac. 'D'you realise that since you went – ?'

It was Fionn's turn to interrupt. 'That Sciabhrach, Fearadach an' Garad are gone to the Other Place? Oh, I know all about that. An' more, too.'

The wind had been well and truly taken out of Cormac's sails. His face showed it. All along the table men leaned forward to get a better view. Fionn's next words they each wanted to listen very carefully to. Fionn, if only they had known it, was bluffing. Yes, he had certainly thought about recent events, for mile upon mile of the road back, but no solution had occurred to him. Still, it was better for a leader to speak out confidently, whether he had anything to say or not. That much he had learned from his father: 'Men respect a firm tongue, boy. Always remember that.'

So he talked, and in spite of himself he noticed that he was beginning to make some kind of sense.

'I was searching my mind these last couple of days to know what could it be that's making the dark of the night so dangerous at Tara, an' only one thing could explain it.'

He stopped. All eyes were on him.

'Go on,' said Taoscán. 'We're listening.'

'I hate to admit it, since I'm the one that brought him here, but it has something to do with that painter.'

He looked at the wall, at the battle-pictures.

'Every man, rest his eyes on them,' he said, sweeping his hand around to include them all, 'an' tell me what ye see.'

'Aren't we gone half-stupid from looking at 'em,' growled Cormac. 'What more is there to see?'

Fionn sat down.

'There's more in it than ye might think' – though for the world he could not see it himself – 'I'm telling ye, look right close at 'em for the time ye're counting to a hundred.'

He sniggered. Few enough in that company would be able to continue counting once they ran out of fingers and toes. But none of them would admit it, he knew, and it would give him a brief space to consult his Thumb of Knowledge. Why he had not done so before was a mystery even to himself. Better late than too late, though.

He planted his chin in his hands, closed his eyes as if he were thinking deeply and behind the clenched fingers slowly began to bite his Thumb. At first there was nothing, but as his teeth clamped tighter a little voice hissed in his head: 'The faces. Where are their faces?'

Fionn stopped breathing. He did not open his eyes. Rather, he bit ever more firmly on the Thumb and silently asked the question, 'Why Fergus?'

And the answer came: 'He knew too much. He knew about the faces.'

Fionn was taking only part of this in. But he knew he must put one last question. There would be no second asking. Three questions only. That was the way of it. And

51

Taoscán would explain the answer later if necessary as he had done so many times before.

'Tell me, Thumb, why did Sciabhrach, Garad, an' Fearadach die? What was it that they knew?'

'Nothing,' whispered the voice. 'Their hair was red. That was it.'

Fionn gasped. His eyes sprang open. Men were still silent, looking at the wall. Only Taoscán observed the change in Fionn. He sat, noting every move while the others stared, scratched their heads, then stared again, all to no avail.

Before Fionn could utter a word Taoscán was on his feet, muttering something in Cormac's ear as he rose. He clenched his throat, smiled.

'Fionn, while men search, as you asked, let us take a walk, you and I, in the cool air. I have a thing or two to say to you on your own.'

'Don't forget to come back an' show us what we're missing here,' from Diarmaid was the only comment voiced at their going.

No sooner were they in the cold dawn outside than the door opened again and they were joined by the king himself.

'There's more going on here than I know about,' he said. 'An' I don't like it. What foolery are you playing at, Fionn? Tell it out to me, an' no more oul' ráiméis from you.'

Fionn began carefully, in a low voice.

'Don't ask me how I know this thing. Only believe that 'tis true. 'Cos that's just what 'tis.'

Cormac gestured impatiently.

'The lad that's gone, I'm afraid he has tuaiplis done on us. 'Twas he killed Fergus. An' he did the same to the others.'

'Why?' Taoscán's question was straight to the point.

Fionn hesitated. 'That's the hard bit. But it had something to do with faces not being there.'

'Where?' – suddenly Taoscán slapped fist into hand, as if he had seen a thing that had long escaped him.

'That's it! I have it.'

Fionn was relieved that at least someone had seen the light. As for himself, all was still as dark as ever.

'Come with me,' Taoscán urged, excited, 'an' I'll show ye.'

He led them in. Men turned in their seats to watch as he walked slowly around, staring intently at all the painted fighting warriors. Several times he nodded, and at last when he addressed the watchers there was surprise as well as annoyance in his voice.

'Isn't is amazing how much a person can look at an' yet see so little.'

Men shuffled, impatient to know what it was that he had seen that they could not.

'Look again,' he began, 'at all those men on the walls.'

They did so.

'How many faces are there?'

There were several gasps of surprise, while other men only stared, dumbfounded that a thing so obvious had escaped them.

'There isn't one face in it, high up or low down,' he continued. 'Now, Fergus noticed that, too, I think, an' that's what cost him his life.'

There was a sudden clatter as a stool was flung back. Dioraing sprang to his feet.

'You could be right, there,' he shouted. All heads swung in his direction. 'I'll never forget, as long as I live, the night Fergus an' myself were on guard-duty an' went into the room above to have a look at how the work was coming on.' He looked nervously at Cormac, not knowing how this might be taken.

'I didn't want anything to do with it, but, sure, ye know the kind of man Fergus was. He was mad anxious to see it. Well I remember him saying there was something missing even though he couldn't exactly say what it was. But that's all I know about it.'

'An' why didn't you talk up before now?' rattled Fionn.

'I was afraid. That's why,' replied Dioraing directly, and they had to be content with that.

'But that doesn't answer our questions,' snorted Cormac. 'Why would he kill Fergus just 'cos he found out that there were no faces in his paintings? That makes no kind of sense.'

'An' what about Fearadach an' the others? Why would he kill them?'

Taoscán was silent. It was Fionn who came to his rescue.

'They all had red hair, hadn't they?' he stated evenly, and brows furrowed as the listeners tried to make sense of this.

'Begor, you're right, Fionn. But we still don't see what that has to do with ...'

Not another word was said, for suddenly Taoscán uttered a little choking cry, swept from the table and rushed towards the door.

Stranger and stranger were the doings of this night becoming. A few moments' silence was followed by a babble of excited voices. What was happening? Where was he gone? Was he sick, or what? Something was seriously amiss, they knew, for never before had Taoscán been seen to move except with a slow dignified tread.

'Sit awhile,' cried Fionn. 'I'll see if he wants any help.'

He would have had fifty willing assistants, but all he wanted was a word of reassurance from Taoscán that things were not as serious as they appeared now to be. He hurried out and came up with the old man near the main gate.

'Don't go out there in the dark of dawn. You would not know what might be waiting to put an end to you.'

Taoscán answered not a word, only signalled the guards to open. They did so at a nod from Fionn, and as they both started down the hill Fionn continued to do all the talking, questioning. But he might as well have been idle for all the satisfaction he got.

Only at the entrance to his own quarters did Taoscán turn and say: 'Fionn, above all else I want quietness. A thought came to me when you mentioned about the red hair, an' if I'm right ... But I must consult my books. I'll be back as soon as I can.'

'Can I give you any help?' Fionn was hoping he might be allowed to stay.

'The best help you can give me now is to keep the crowd above quiet. Why don't you tell 'em a story or something like that? I won't be long doing what I have to ... because I have a fair idea of what I'm looking for.'

And with that he closed Fionn out.

THERE WAS NO NEED for Fionn to entertain or amuse the crowd in the hall. As he paused just outside the door, wondering what he would say, he heard the buzz of talk from inside.

'There's no shortage of entertainment in there, whatever else,' he mused. Yet when he tried to enter without being noticed the conversation instantly died.

'Any news, Fionn? Where's Taoscán? Has he the

story for us?' and fifty other questions were fired at him all at once.

'He'll answer all ye have to ask when he comes in himself. He said he won't be long, so have a bit of patience if ye can.'

'But tell us ...'

'I can tell ye nothing. He's the one that'll do the talking. As ye well know, he's able to explain himself better than any man walking.'

It hardly pleased them, this, but it was all they got.

When Taoscán came in shortly afterwards there was a pallor on his cheeks that was more pronounced than usual. They studied him closely as he took his place near Cormac, but only those nearest to him noticed that his hands shook. Fionn was one of them.

'That's no good omen,' he whispered to Oisín. 'Get ready to hear bad news.'

'I won't stand up, men, while I talk,' Taoscán began. 'The weight of what I have to say is too heavy on me.'

All who heard these words bit their lips, shifted nervously and waited. Taoscán looked at Cormac, who nodded him on.

'Ye might remember me saying that when the painter showed me the picture he had of his master I recognised the face from somewhere.'

They nodded, whether they remembered or not.

'Well, I was right. Now I know who that man was. Oh, an' well I do.'

He said the words with heavy regret, maybe even bitterness. No one interrupted him, tried to hurry him on, though most of them would have wished to.

'Draointeoir. That's who was in it.'

'Who's he?' they asked each other. 'We never heard the name before now.'

'An' ye're not a bit the worse for that, I can tell ye. He was the worst, the evillest-minded gruagach I met in forty years of going to druids' meetings. An' the great pity of it all was that he had a mind as sharp as a scian. There was nothing he couldn't do when he put that mind to it.'

'But what happened that made him turn bad?'

'That's a question we talked over time out of mind, an' we never came to any proper answer for it, even though I have my own ideas about it.'

'Dhera,' said Diarmaid, 'you'd often hear stories of great men going astray after a belt on the head in battle.'

'Or from falling down after a big feed of uisce beatha,' chimed in Conán Maol helpfully.

''Twas nothing like that,' said Taoscán. 'Pride that did it, if anything. I heard him once to say that some day he'd rule the four corners of the world. But when Fear Feasa, our chief druid, heard those foolish words he ordered him to get down on his knees and lick the dust of the ground to cure his ambition. He did it, too. But I'll never forget the look he gave Fear Feasa when he got up. An' the same man didn't live long afterwards, either.'

'What d'ye do with him?' asked Fionn, surprised. He had not heard this story before despite all the years he had known Taoscán.

'He was barred from coming to any of our meetings for seven years, but to my mind that was no punishment. It only gave him freedom an' time to brew badness. He never came near any of us after the seven years were up. So of course we forgot about him. 'Twas as if the ground swallowed him. An' to tell the truth 'twas only when I saw that picture that he came to my mind again.'

'How long ago did all that happen?' asked Goll, obviously interested.

'Ah, it must be ... all of forty-five years ago, I s'pose. Half a lifetime, Goll.'

And there the questions ended for a while. They could think of nothing more to ask until Fionn suddenly recalled the hair. Anything to keep the silence at bay.

'You said something to me a while ago about the red hair, Taoscán,' he offered.

'Indeed I did. An' that's the very thing that has me worried.'

He looked around. Everyone was watching him.

'Ye all know well enough that red-haired people are close related to the slua sí.'

Heads nodded.

'Well, if Draointeoir sent out the lad that was here to bring away their faces, he has a good reason for it. He must need 'em to work magic. An' if I know him it'll be to no one's advantage but his own. He won't be happy until he has the world in his fist. He said as much himself. An' I have no doubt that this picture of the world I was told about is part of the plan.'

'An' is there any way to stop him?' It was Cormac who spoke. He did not relish the prospect of giving up his power to a painter of pictures from a forest in Thuringia, however skilful he might be.

'The first thing to be done is follow that lad an' bring him back. Maybe we could put some kind of a squeeze on him to tell us whatever he knows.'

'I'll do more than squeeze him when I lay my hands on him,' Fionn hissed grimly, remembering Sciabhrach and the others. 'He'll never see his forest again, that's one thing sure.'

'I'll leave all that to you; only make sure you don't damage him until I can have words with him – an' be careful to bring his pack back with you, too. Secrets or no secrets, I'm going to open those two jars this time. If the world an' ourselves are in danger all means must be allowed us to keep the bad thing from us.'

This was the kind of talk Fionn liked to hear. No more being gentle with the villain, only get out there and drag him back, by the heels if needs be. Then to work on his secrets and ... heh! ... possibilities began to open up in his mind, and for the first time that day he smiled.

'When can we go?' he asked Taoscán impatiently, then turning to the men, 'an' which of ye is coming with me to catch him?'

A forest of hands rose as one and the clamour of voices was joined by a hammering of fists on tables. Fionn was pleased with the response. No cowardice there, anyway. Taoscán stood now and signalled for quiet.

'I won't tell ye when to go, but the sooner the better. He's putting distance between himself an' us with every minute that passes. An' he's in a great hurry. I know that much for sure.'

This was as good as telling them to start at once. And that is exactly what they did, stampeded to the door and crashed out into the brightening day.

'Get the dogs!' Fionn ordered, and they were brought, yelping, straining against their handlers, full of excitement and eager to be on the scent. But before they started Fionn had an announcement to make.

'Men, there's no sense in all of us going, leaving Ireland unguarded. An' there's no fear that King Cormac'd allow it, anyway. Some of ye must stay here for fear the thing that's killing by night comes back.'

A deafening silence greeted these words.

'Isn't that one of the main reasons we want to be gone out of this place,' whispered Goll to his brother, Conán. Fionn heard the remark. It was time for action, he knew.

'Muise, Goll, I knew you'd be the first to volunteer for the dangerous task. You'll have his majesty's gratitude for this, I can tell you.'

Goll spluttered a few words of protest, but he was caught. He could not pull back now, in front of all his companions. His honour would be in tatters, as Fionn well knew. Then Taoscán, to take the sting out of it, added: 'An' I have a good strong potion on my shelf that'll keep ye awake even if ye have to wait a whole week for the beast to come. So don't have any fears that ye'll be killed while ye're asleep.'

'Fears?' bristled Goll. 'I'm afraid of no ollpiast, gruagach or monster. Let him come by night or day, I'll face him.'

'Pick whatever men you want with you, so, an' we'll start,' said Fionn. 'Time or that boyo won't wait for us.'

BY FORCED MARCHES THEY reached the sea-shore by midmorning, stopping only to enquire here and there whether the stranger had passed that way. Everyone seemed to have noticed him: 'The lad with the bag, is it? Oh, he passed there below not so long ago.'

'Yes. He was there at the well looking for a drink of water.'

'The thing I noticed about him was that he had no weapons. What kind of a man could that be?'

They tracked him all the way to Beann Éadair, where they were told that he had taken ship for the world beyond the eastern horizon: 'Dar fia, but he had the choice of any ship he wanted, with the bag of gold he was offering.'

'I hope Cormac had his treasure-chest clamped tight,' was Fionn's suspicious comment when he heard this.

Within an hour they were themselves on the waves,

all sails hoisted and in hot pursuit. And lack of wind was no hindrance, for whenever it died down, Fionn gave orders that a dozen men at a time should brace themselves together in the stern and blow with all their might. Once or twice the captain had to curb their enthusiasm, when they were in danger of flittering the sails or bending the mast to breaking-point, but he was impressed by their performance, all the same.

'If it ever happens that ye're out of work, men, come to me first. I won't see ye short.'

And to show his admiration and goodwill, he would take no passage-money when at last they beached in England.

'What's more,' he said, 'I'll be here again this time next week if ye want a way home.'

And with those words he waved them out of sight.

All that day they marched through Cumbria, admiring the countryside, wishing they had the leisure to see it at their own pace. But even when deer and wild boar sprang up before and beside them, then sprinted away, they did not give chase, though many a time they were mortally tempted. Fionn kept them in check, reminding them of the serious business in hand: 'Take no notice of them. It could all be a trick of that cursed bodach to put us out of our way.'

'I hope that's the truth of it,' replied Conán. 'Otherwise the men of this part of the world, whatever 'tis called, don't deserve the fine country they have. Anyone that wouldn't be out hunting every day in a place like this must either be short of brains or legs.'

They travelled on, consoling themselves with the promise that they would certainly return, and as darkness closed around them that evening Fionn spoke gravely: 'It wouldn't surprise me a bit if that lad tried to do us harm in the night. So let the guards watch closely for him two by two. Call me if anything stirs.'

With that they settled down around the fire, weapons close to hand, guards and dogs alert for any movements in the dark. Hour followed hour without interruption and at last even the dogs began to nod off. But some time in the deepest silence before dawn, Fionn – probably in the middle of a dream – rolled over awkwardly and on to the hilt of his sword. It winded him. He sat up with a grunt, muttered and rubbed his back.

And then he saw it! A thing flitting from shade to shadow at the edge of the camp. Where were the guards, the dogs? Asleep by the sound of them – he could hear various snores and snorts. But he did not panic. He had served in danger too often for that. Better to let the enemy show himself, if indeed it was an enemy. He sank back on to his rolled-up cloak, fingering his dagger.

Yes. There it was again, a figure, and resembling a person. He had not been mistaken. He watched it break soundlessly from the darkness and pad, silent, into the dull glow of the campfire-embers. His fingers tightened on the knife as the thing picked its way steadily towards ... himself, then paused a moment over him. Fionn could see no face, but all his senses tingled as the shadowed figure raised a dark claw from the folds of its clothing. It hovered an instant over his head, the long nails glistening dimly. Then it swooshed down. Fionn could hear the slight hiss as it closed with him. He jerked himself sideways, faster than he could ever remember moving in his life, stabbing upward at the thing as he moved.

He was on his feet like lightning, shouting and slashing at the same time, but in the few seconds it took dogs and men to gather themselves around him it was gone. Vanished. Without a trace. No one else had seen it except

Fionn. But they knew from his face, when torches had been lit, that they had had a narrow escape from some evil thing. He explained nothing for a few moments, until he had examined the ground all about. There were no tracks. Nothing.

'That was no dream, whatever else it was,' he declared to the silent watchers as well as to himself.

'Are you going to leave us here long more, wondering?' broke in Liagán. 'What was it you saw?'

'A black claw,' he said simply. 'An' only that I moved when I did I'd have no face on me now.'

He had the words out before he understood their full sense.

'Dar Crom,' he breathed, 'my face could be gone by that evil beast, just like the other poor misfortunates.'

'A pity you didn't get a hold on him, an' we'd make short work of him,' snarled Diarmaid.

'I'm not too sure ye would,' sighed Fionn, 'because I put this knife here up an' out through him, an' still no sign of blood or nothing. It was like I'd be trying to cut the air.'

This news did nothing to encourage them back to sleep. They talked away what remained of the night in nervous little groups, each one of them relieved when at last dawn put the shadows to flight.

They ate, without much enthusiasm, and were only too glad to leave that particular place behind them, and as they tramped on and considered how close they had come to a horrible end, their admiration of the country and their enthusiasm seemed to wither. Fionn noticed this.

'Don't look so worried, men! As soon as we catch him he'll be the one with the long face – as well as one claw missing.'

All his attempts to cheer them fell on deaf ears, however, and he had given it up as a bad job long before they reached a bare range of hills at dusk.

'What place is this, I wonder?' asked Oisín.

'There's one way to find out,' replied Diarmaid. 'Look at that house there, beyond. We can enquire there.'

They did so, and the old woman who answered their knock seemed startled to see them.

'God bless an' save me,' said she, 'but what's taking everyone along this road today? Is there a fair or a battle beyond the hills?'

'Everyone?' enquired Fionn. 'Who was here before us?'

'There was a man, sir. One man. But that's more than I meet here usually in the length of a month.'

'When did he pass?'

'Two hours ago, maybe.'

Fionn pursed his lips and glanced at the others.

'We won't catch him tonight,' shrugged Diarmaid, 'an' that's a bare an' lonely spot we're facing. Tell us, old woman, what name is on these hills?'

'The Hills of Pennine,' she replied. 'Surely ye're not thinking of crossing over there in the night? I wouldn't advise it. Many a good man – my own husband among 'em – met 'is end out there in the dark of the night an' was never found after. There's creatures out there ...'

'We know that,' said Fionn, 'an' that's why I'm asking you now can we stay the night here?'

'Ye're more than welcome, 'cos ye have honest faces at least, not like that other one who called.'

'What did he look like?' asked Fionn, curious to know their enemy for when they should meet again.

'That I can't tell you. He came no farther than the door there an' with the light at 'is back I couldn't see 'is face. But the voice of 'im made me shiver. There was frost an' ice in it, an' something worse, too. 'E's not a man I'd like to 'ave much to do with, an' that's why I'm glad to 'ave ye 'ere.'

'What did he want? Did he ask for anything?'

'Only to know the fastest way across the hills. That an' a drink of water.'

'An' tell me,' said Fionn, as they settled themselves around the hearth, 'is there any other way over that might be even shorter than the one you showed him?'

'Indeed there is, an' several. But be prepared for 'ardship if ye follow those tracks. They're made by goats for goats, an' not for people.'

'We'll do our best, whatever they're like. We have to get in front of that lad before he reaches the eastern sea, or else we'll never catch him.'

In the ashes from the hearth with a piece of stick she drew for them a map of the land about, and they could only marvel at the detail of her knowledge. Every hillock and stream was there, it seemed, and all the pathways, big and small. Fionn could not help but comment on her remarkable skill: 'I don't know how you can remember 'em all, good woman, but you seem to know your way around here, whatever else.'

'Ah, young man, if you 'ad as much time spent 'ere alone as I 'ave, you'd know the place too. Either that or you'd be gone into a vegetable. An' I won't go among strangers now, not in the small time that's left to me.'

Fionn nodded. He could sympathise with that. It would be his very own reaction, he knew.

None of them slept that night either, only brooded over the paths she had drawn for them, memorising them, every one, for they realised that on knowing them might depend their very lives on the morrow.

WHAT LITTLE FOOD SHE had she shared with them at breakfast, then pointing them towards a distant eastern hill she said – 'Get to that by midday and 'e won't be much before ye.'

A last shake-hands, a wave, and they were away, anxious to lose no minute that would help narrow the distance between themselves and him.

But so great was his impatience that Fionn gave an order that he was quickly to regret – 'An slí díreach, men! Straight on for that hill.'

Diarmaid looked askance at him.

'After all our talk last night? 'Tisn't like Fionn to lose his head. I hope he has knowledge that's hidden from the rest of us.'

That he had no such knowledge was quickly proven, for in the space of five hundred paces they had gone to their waists in a dark, menacing mire and were in danger of being swallowed entirely.

'I think we'd be better to stop an' go back to the way the oul' woman told us, Fionn,' suggested Liagán gently, nervous of what the reaction might be. But Fionn, if he was even listening, had arrived at some similar conclusion. He stood a moment, only half visible now, holding some silent conversation with himself, then waved them backwards, to where they had started from. No easy job that was, for the ooze had taken a close liking to them and seemed most anxious to hold them in its sticky grip. On solid ground at last almost an hour later, exhausted by the effort, Fionn observed: 'If I didn't know better – an' I don't – I'd say that blackguard ahead of us put that stuff there to hold us back,' but that attempt at wisdom convinced no one.

'We'll go the ways she told us, Fionn,' said Liagán, 'an' at least we'll get to where we're going.'

There was no further argument. Time was against them now and as they squinted at the sun it was obvious to one and all that if they were to reach the hill by the time advised they would need to hurry. That they arrived, and even with a little time to spare, was mainly due to Liagán Luaimneach's sure foot and exact memory for detail. Even Fionn managed his version of a gruff 'thanks' when he said: 'We must keep you in mind, Liagán, the next time we're going to the Other World. You'd make a great guide back.'

At the top of Mickle Fell they rested, silently scanning the land eastward as they did so. Nothing was moving.

'Blast it,' snarled Fionn, 'we must have missed him, however it happened.'

''Twas that pádáiling in the bog that did it,' said Feardorcha rattily. 'Now what'll we do? He could be anywhere.'

It was a conversation that might have led to bad feelings, or even blows, had not Diarmaid at that moment half-idly turned to look down the hill and back the way they had just come. He gaped.

'By the left leg of Lugh,' he whispered, 'look what's coming, will ye.'

Every head turned. There, maybe a mile off, they saw a man approaching, and it was obvious from even that distance that he was both laden and in a hurry.

'Hah! Look at the gimp of him. There's no mistaking who that is, anyway,' said Fionn. 'It must be the bag that delayed him.'

'Whatever it was, we'd better keep down or he'll see us if he looks up,' was Liagán's sensible comment.

They threw themselves into the heather and from that vantage-point watched him approach, several of them unable to keep from sniggering at the thought of the shock he would get on being unexpectedly confronted in that bare place. Little they realised that it was they who were in for a shock, for he was no more than a hundred paces away when he stopped, swung the pack from his shoulder and fingered it open as speedily as if his life itself depended on it.

'What's the cursed fellow doin' now?' whispered Feardorcha, mystified.

As they watched, a handful of the little stone pots were snatched out and opened in almost the same movement by the artist, and then, before their amazed eyes, he proceeded to paint himself from their view with a few rapid strokes of a tiny brush that had appeared in his hand as if by magic.

They could not understand it. Goggle-eyed, they rose from where they lay and stood dumbly.

'I'd feel a lot safer if we had Taoscán here with us now, Diarmaid,' nodded Fionn. 'How do we know what that bodach is goin' to do next?'

'It'll be nothing good for us, anyway,' replied Diarmaid.

It was a fear they were all wrestling with, for they were at his mercy, now that he was invisible, and well they knew it. Dry lips were licked while they waited for the worst to happen.

Conán was first to crack.

'Look, I'm not stopping here to be mauled like Sciabhrach an' the rest of 'em while my legs are still working,' and before they could call him, stop him, accuse him of cowardice or anything else, he was leaping madly away through the heather.

But not for long. In his fright he had not considered the true lie of the ground and was gone only a few steps when he flaked his left big toe against a hidden rock, shattering the nail. He crumpled at once in a ball of pain, rolling, clutching and cursing. When he righted himself, moaning, his first concern was for the broken nail. But not for that part that still remained with his toe. What exercised him was the piece that had vanished into the heather. For the thought was with him now, the memory of his grandfather's warning all those years ago: 'Don't let no one get a hold of a hair of your head or a nail of your finger or toe. Burn 'em if you have to get rid of 'em but don't let 'em out of your sight.'

Gruagachs, well he knew, had gained power over many a strong man by means of those simple things. Great warriors had been turned to giggling simpletons by a single snaidhm of a beard-hair, fearless axe-men reduced to witless wrecks by the chopping-up of a captive nail. And he was not going to risk that happening to him, no matter what. So he fell to his knees and scrabbled furiously in the heather.

The others gaped stupidly at him, not knowing what to make of this sudden fit of his. As far as they could see, not alone was something wrong – everything seemed to be going astray, and at the most unfortunate time possible. Fionn decided that it was his duty to intervene. These antics were for another place, not now.

'Rise out of that, Conán,' he said. 'Enough is enough. We have a job on our hands an' all you can do is ...'

He never finished, for Conán stiffened at that instant, his gaze fixed on the air, it seemed, to the left of Fionn's shoulder and above it. His lips moved, his eyes bulged; he tried to speak but failed. All he could do at last was beckon Fionn to him by a faint motioning of his little finger, and the look of panic on his face was enough to convince Fionn that this was no foolery. He leaned down.

'What's on you, Conán? Why in the name of Torna are you looking out over my shoulder? What is it you see?'

Conán signalled him closer, then whispered urgently in his ear: 'He's there! Standing not six feet to the west of you. I can see him from here clear against the sky.'

Fionn pulled away sharply.

'What're you talking about? Are your senses leaving you? I see no one.'

Conán's frightened eyes darted back and forth.

'Well, if you were here where I am maybe you would,' he snorted, and so saying he sprang suddenly, lithe as a cat, brushing Fionn aside, his hairy arms arcing out, snatching.

All those standing by were even more dumbfounded than before. Poor Conán! After all his noble deeds, all the brawls and battles he had survived, to end so, rolling like a foolish pup through the heather on a foreign hillside. Sad, sad.

But Conán was feeling no such grief. As his fingers locked on their prey he shrieked in triumph: 'I have the cursed devil! Hold him! Jump on him, quick before he gets away again.'

They may not have had the proof of their eyes to go by, but the edge in his voice was enough to move them to act. As one they threw themselves on where they reckoned whatever it was he was holding must be. And sure enough they connected with the limbs of a person. A brief hard struggle, and all was still.

'Bring him down here to this pool below an' we'll see who we have,' panted Fionn.

'No need to ask that,' grinned Conán. 'I can tell ye. 'Tis our own good friend the painter.'

'Well, well!' said Diarmaid, 'isn't it us that's the lucky

70

lads, to meet such an interesting man again,' giving the leg he was holding a sharp twist. And then for the first time since he had left Tara they heard the voice of their invisible enemy, a cry of anger and pain: 'Let go of me this minute or you are dead. Every man of you.'

Far from doing anything of the sort they lugged him to the stream, held securely all the while to what they could feel of him, and let the water do its work. The result was indeed what they had hoped for. Bit by gradual bit, as the paint he had so quickly applied was washed away, he became visible, and never did man return to the seen world to a more eager welcome than he now received. A circle of yellow-toothed grins hemmed him in. Hairy fingers clasped him even more tightly now that their owners could see what it was they were holding.

'If it isn't yourself, 'tis your brother that's in it, surely,' smiled Fionn, 'but it don't matter a bit as long as you're with us when we arrive back at Tara. There's people there that want to do a powerful lot of talking to you.'

The captive glowered at them, viciousness in his eyes.

'I am warning you, what I said I meant. Every one of you that has a hand on me now will die in agony. I have my master's word behind me when I say that. His work must be done, and *will* be.'

Fionn pushed his face close up to the other's and rasped between gritted teeth: 'That might look to you like a good plan, you feallaire, but you'll have time enough to be thinking of a new one on the way back to Tara with us,' and without more ado he gave gruff and firm orders: 'Bind him – tight – an' don't let him out of sight for an instant. I'll scalp the man that lets him escape.'

He need have had no fears on that score. By the time

Liagán and Conán finished the pleasant task of tying and knotting, the artist was able to move his eye-brows but little besides. They hoisted him then, and just to be on the safe side, rammed him head-first into Fionn's hunting-sack. If he was not secure in that there was security nowhere within the four corners of the world. And the more he struggled the better they liked it.

'Time for him to get a bit of hardship, the lúbaire.'

'An' he'll get worse than that if he keeps up his útamáiling,' said Fionn, and then more softly, 'I'd trample him into the ground an' get pleasure from it only that he's wanted back at Tara. An' that's where we'll take him now, with no more delay, either.'

They were all only too prepared to agree with that. Conán was especially pleased, his sore toe quite forgotten now, for he knew that there would be honourable mention of him when the story came to be told in the great hall. After all, but for him it was likely that *they* would all now be in the artist's pack, and on their way to the dark vastness of Thuringia.

IF EVER A HURRICANE blew across the Irish Sea it was after that same excited group boarded the ship that was waiting for them, just as the good captain had promised it would be. First they fell to and manned the oars, but that was too slow for their taste, so anxious were they to be home and displaying their prize. So they trooped, every man of them, to the stern of the ship, and this time no one had to be told by Fionn what to do; in fact, he joined them himself, and such a terrific gale did they raise up that the waves and white foam fled in terror before them and they were sucked along at a dizzy speed and in a flurry of spray and spatters. Timber and canvas were tested that day to their breaking-point, and it was just as well that the captain, expecting something like this, had taken the precaution of investing in new masts and sails, because by the time Beann Éadair came into view a mere two hours later the same masts were bent almost level with the deck and the sails were swelled to the size of Conán Maol's belly after one of his voracious sprees of gluttony.

'Ho! Ye can stop now, men,' roared the captain, holding on for dear life to the gunwale. There was no let-up.

'In the name of Crom, stop! Or we'll end up above on top of the headland, or buried in it.'

He screamed the words this time, and they seemed to have the desired effect. They stopped blowing and, like magic, the sea became calm. But the storm they had sent before them tore on inland, uprooting trees, lifting houses and ricks of hay and sweeping people and cattle into the air as far away as Connacht.

Their attention, however, was all on the shore now directly before them, and as soon as the ship screeched to a halt at the foot of the cliff and well above high-water mark they leaped overboard, shouted fond farewells to the bemused captain and rushed off towards the Boyne and Tara.

'Rot an' blast it,' shouted the poor man at their backs, 'but what good is my ship to me beached up here?' and he and his crew set out at once after them.

The trail they left was easy to follow, too, for in their hurry they threw care to the winds. All that mattered now was to get their prisoner delivered as quickly as might be.

THE GATES OF TARA stood open wide to receive them. They had been seen afar off by the sentries and the word had quickly spread so that by the time they set foot on the Hill a large crowd stood waiting to greet them. In front of all was Cormac and a worried-looking Taoscán who said, before Fionn could speak a word or give any explanation of anything – 'Did ye bring the pack?'

A tense pause. Then Fionn smiled triumphantly.

'We did. An' himself as well.'

'Good. Give it here to me. An' take him down to the Black Hole – if that's as your highness would have it.'

This last was addressed with a little smile to Cormac, a sop to his pride, but all knew that he could not object. If Taoscán did not know what he was doing now, God help them all when the artist was let out of the bag and came fully to himself.

'Do it,' Cormac ordered the guards shortly. 'But keep him in the bag until we get down ourselves.'

Even as they clattered off Taoscán was fingering the pack.

'This time there'll be no secrets. Whatever it is that's in the two jars, I'm going to open 'em.'

It was Liagán who once again interrupted with a sensible suggestion.

'Why don't you do it below where he is? That way we could watch what happens an' maybe find out once an' for all what 'tis he's hiding.'

'The very thing,' replied Taoscán. 'The same thought was in my own head.'

Accompanied by guards with torches they carried the pack down the forty-two steps to the Black Hole, but no one was allowed to enter the chamber itself except Fionn, Taoscán and Cormac. There was room for no one else, in any case.

The artist was sitting in the farthest-off corner, picking his nose. He did not stop when they trooped in, only raised an eyebrow scornfully in their direction, then flicked something – they could guess what – towards them. Fionn clenched his fists.

'You low savage. If you can't show respect for the King of Ireland I won't feel too bad about making small pieces of you here an' now,' and he would have done so had not Taoscán restrained him with a few quiet words.

'No, Fionn. This time is mine. You did all you had to by bringing him here. Leave this part of it to me.'

Without more delay he held out the pack and smiled gently.

'This is yours, I think.'

All the insolence left the other's face. He scrambled to his feet.

'It is. And you have no right to it. Give it to me at once!'

He sprang forward and might have snatched it, but it was no longer there. Taoscán had tossed it sideways to Cormac, who now began deliberately, steadily, to untie the thong that bound it. Fionn stood, rock-like, itching for a chance to flatten the villain if only he tried once more to intervene.

But there was no intervention. The artist seemed to freeze as Cormac's fingers loosened the knots. His mouth sagged. He shrank back, pawing the stones of the wall nervously as the two mystery jars were placed, together with all the others, on the floor.

There was silence when Cormac straightened at last. Then Taoscán said quietly, 'This is the end of it. An' I'm sorry we never even found out your name in all the time you were with us. But, sure, 'tis easy to be wise after the worst is done – though you can still tell us, if you like.'

But never a word answered this kindly offer, so with a shrug he began to uncork the jars, one after another, until only the two were left. It was clear to all that here was the nub of the whole ugly matter.

Taoscán tried one last gesture of helpfulness.

'D'you want to tell us what's in 'em? Wouldn't you have sense an' not be making things awkward for all of us.'

No reply from the artist, only a twisting of his mouth into an ugly grimace and a rasping 'pthu' as he lobbed a spit at Taoscán's feet. He was about to follow this with words, but in two steps Fionn was beside him, snarling. His hands swung out and up, connected with the other's ribs and swept him back as if he were a leaf. He struck the wall, seemed to hang there a moment, part of it, and then slithered on to the floor.

'Easy, Fionn. Easy!' Taoscán warned. 'Don't kill him. We might need him yet.'

'He's a dirty animal, that's what he is. An' if what's inside in the crocks is anything like him we'd be better to leave 'em as they are an' fire 'em out into the sea.'

Taoscán paid no attention. He was already busy with the cork of the first jar. A few seconds of effort and it came away in his hand. He grunted, smiled briefly, then squinted into the little circle of darkness. His smile died. The jar was empty!

'What – ?'

He would have said more, but his attention was drawn to the artist, who had just dragged himself into a sitting position and was holding his hands out, trembling, pleading, though no words came. The fear in his ashen face was more eloquent than anything he might have said.

Cormac stood over him.

'What's the meaning of this oul' acting? If there's nothing in 'em why were you keeping 'em secret? Is it so you were going to put *us* into 'em, or what, hah?'

Taoscán was prying off the other cork even as the king spoke. And it was then the artist's voice came to him, but only as a cracked whisper.

'Don't! Leave it on, or they'll get out!'

'They? Who's "they"?'

'We'll find out now – in spite of him,' sighed Taoscán as the cork popped off and rattled, unnaturally loudly, into a corner.

All of what happened next they could, none of them, bring to mind clearly afterwards. But they were to remember all their days the sharp sucking noise, the belch of white, then black, smoke, hands clawing up out of one jar, then the other, elbows levering bodies out, heads, shoulders and more. But something, they saw at once, was very wrong, for not one of all those men, each one of them red-haired, had a face!

And the darkness that fell on the room then, it too they would recall, for it gathered itself around them like a tight-fitting garment and squeezed at their throats, their chests, until they were aware of nothing of the bedlam that now broke loose in that narrow place. They staggered back, all except Taoscán, whose experience of the powers of darkness now stood him and all of them in good stead. He began to chant in a voice that threw up a thin wall of safety to cover their escape. Yet even he soon began to back away, his hands rigid as spears before him, like the rearguard of an army withdrawing from mortal danger.

Outside he found the corridor empty. Cormac and all the rest had removed themselves with wonderful haste. He could hear the last of their footsteps battering the steps far above. He sighed, then concentrated all his attention on the curls of smoke that had begun to inch cautiously around the door-jambs of the cell.

'Here it must be stopped, if that gets out into the light of day we'll never have peace in the land again.' So saying he breathed deeply, closed his eyes and seemed to shrink into himself as he summoned to him every one of the powers of goodness that were capable of being commanded.

'Lugh! Lugh! Bright one, come. If ever your people needed help 'tis now ... now ... now ...'

He felt himself swoon as those words echoed down through his very being, out, out, and swirled into the vastness of the Mind beyond Mind, a forlorn little cry from the world of men.

And then ... then, in the silence began a rustling, like leaves in a breeze, like birds far away, like many voices in a mighty shout all together, rising, rising. He clapped his hands to his ears as a huge chorus billowed and swelled and broke around him, words, words, and a music that was beyond the knowing of human ears.

He fell. And above him Tara shook in unison with the shivering of the very air. Men cringed into corners, hid in the nearest dark places. Even Fionn believed that the world was breaking into its last pieces. The palace gates rattled, slabs of plaster were shaken from the wall and a huge split crackled open all across the courtyard.

'We're doomed!' bawled Feardorcha. 'Why didn't we leave that dirty devil where he was an' stay across the sea ourselves while we had the chance?'

'It don't look too good, right enough,' muttered Fionn, his hands over his head.

'Never mind that,' cried Liagán, the sensible one. 'What about poor Taoscán? Are ye forgetting that he's still down below in that place? If he's killed we'll all be done for – an' our honour, too. We'll be remembered as cowards, an' nothing else.'

No response. No move.

'If that's the way ye want men to think of ye, well an' good. I'll take *my* chances below,' and he leaped forward, towards the door and the stairs down.

His words had an immediate effect. As one, the others sprang from their cringeing-places, remembering now that they were no less than the Fianna of Éireann, that it was their duty to be strong and brave even if the sky were collapsing in lumps about their heads. And, by Crom, that much they would do, no matter that they had to die for it!

The door disintegrated, terrified, into matchwood ever before their hurtling shoulders connected with it, and they piled into the hallway and squeezed to the trapdoor leading to the Black Hole. It was lying skew-wise, thrown as the escapees had left it in their rush to get out.

'Be careful,' whispered Fionn. 'No knowing what's lurking down there,' and he cautiously edged nearer, peering into the pitch-black space.

'Taoscán!' he called softly.

No reply.

'Taoscán! Are you there?' This time he almost shouted, but only the echo of his voice came back, taunting.

'We'll have to go down there again,' he said, his voice taut. 'Whether we like it or not.'

No one disagreed. Nor did anyone volunteer to be first to descend. Fionn sighed. He knew that he, as always, must do the necessary and remembered his father's words – 'If you won't do it yourself don't ask your men to do it either.'

'All right,' he breathed. 'Stay here. I'll be back ... maybe.'

He stepped cautiously down, feeling his way one tip-toe at a time, his dagger at the ready. There would be little space to swing his great sword down here, and well he knew it. The little dagger would do just as well, he decided, for whatever he might encounter.

Forty-two steps in that darkness was almost more than even his iron nerves could bear, and several times he stopped to listen. But always he was greeted by silence, a hollowness that seemed spiked with claws, every one ready to lunge at him.

Step by slow step he inched his way down until he was sure he was at the bottom. Only the little corridor lay between him and the cell door now, he knew, but what might it contain? He licked his dry lips, took a step forward – and connected with something soft, fleshy. Like lightning he drew back, all his senses tingling for the attack he had been expecting. Swaying gently from side to side, his dagger cutting a half-circle around him, he waited for the worst. When nothing happened he reached his left hand down cautiously and began to explore the thing on the floor. Clothing ... long hair ... the features of a face ... beard. His mouth clapped shut as realisation dawned on him. Taoscán! And he was dead! It was that first terrible thought that brought his voice to him in a shout that made the darkness shudder.

'Lights down here, quick! Taoscán is murdered, or maybe worse.'

He was on his knees now, and cradling the still figure in his arms, fumbling for a pulse or any other sign of life. There was none.

'Dar an Tiarna Geal,' he whispered, almost crying, 'don't die on us, Taoscán. The place wouldn't stand long without you.'

It was then that the first of the men thundered down the stairs, torch flaming, scattering silence and darkness together in his hurry. Light spilled on to the still form of

Taoscán as one after another they tightened into a circle around him. Cormac pushed his way forward and threw himself onto his knees beside Fionn.

'How is he?'

Fionn never took his eyes off Taoscán's still face, only shook his head and then let it slump into his hand.

'It can't be!' said Cormac in a horrified whisper. 'Not now, surely.'

He was, perhaps, thinking of how he, as well as all the rest, had deserted Taoscán when help was needed.

Fionn, in a frenzy, lifted his old friend into a sitting position and shook him.

'Come back, Taoscán. You're not going to leave us at the mercy of them murdering demons, are you?'

He shook him again.

'Leave it, Fionn,' sighed Cormac. 'There's nothing more we can do here ... except ...'

Fionn glared up, a look of disgust on his face.

'No. I won't leave him. How could I, after all he did for me, an' for every one of us, since we came here?'

He turned his attention again on Taoscán's unmoving face, then – blinding flash of insight – thought of his oxter-bag! His hand streaked to it, fumbled with the cords and plunged in. It was out as quickly, and Fionn found himself staring at a large shrivelled leaf, ugly, dark and strong-smelling. Without a second thought, as if knowing exactly what to do, he clapped it over Taoscán's face. Within two seconds the old man shuddered, heaved, then flung his arms out and sat up clawing for the thing that was smothering him. He snatched it away, and there he was, their old friend, most certainly alive, wheezing and coughing.

'Akhh!' he spluttered. 'Is it trying to kill me you are, Fionn?'

But all the same he smiled, a smile that was contagious. Soon everyone standing there was either sighing with relief or laughing, shaking Taoscán's hand or trying to question him, all at once.

Cormac took command then and saw that Taoscán's energies might be needed for more serious matters.

'Quiet! Let him get his breath at least, will ye. Time for questions later.'

He turned to Taoscán: 'Are you well enough, d'you think, to face that place there?' His finger stabbed towards the cell door.

There was not even the shadow of a tremor in Taoscán's voice as he replied – 'As well as I need to be to do it.'

He rose stiffly, then turned, and very deliberately paced the six steps to the door, followed silently by the rest, their torches making as much smoke as light now. At the threshold he stopped, beckoned them to be still, then listened intently, brow furrowed, head inclined to one side. A few seconds of this, then he stepped into that dark place.

Goll glanced at Fionn, uncertain whether to follow.

'Go on,' said Fionn simply. 'I'm here behind you.'

They entered, and almost collided with Taoscán, who was standing motionless just within. He was muttering to himself, something they did not catch – or try to, for the sight that greeted them took all words from them.

From top to bottom the brightly-painted walls were spattered with blood. Flung about were the torn remains of what had been a person, fingers here, a leg there, tatters of clothing and skin, hair in tufts. And fragments of crushed bones. It was more than any of them could look on for long.

'Come out of it,' cried Fionn, 'before I get sick. It

looks the nearest thing I ever saw to a slaughterhouse.'

They retreated, disgusted, babbling among themselves of the horribleness of the scene.

It was a few minutes before Taoscán joined them in the corridor but when he did it was obvious that he had something serious to say. Cormac held up his hand.

'Hush, men, an' maybe we'll find out the start an' finish of this misfortunate work.'

All attention on him, Taoscán spoke at last. 'Ye saw what's inside here?'

Heads nodded.

'It isn't pleasing to look at, is it?'

Every head shook.

'Well, we're lucky that there isn't worse to pay than that, bad an' all as 'tis. This fellow inside was wrapped up in evil work, an' he came very near to bringing the curse of Balor down on top of us.'

They shuddered, those fearless men, at the thought of the burning and roasting that might have been their lot, and listened, fascinated, for the next revelation.

'I'm sorry that he came to such a bad end,' said Taoscán, 'but many's the time I saw the self-same thing – a man that'd be doing well, going up in the world bit by bit, an' all of a sudden he'd get a notion that he was bigger than the times he was living in. Nothing for him then only the stars.'

His voice dropped.

''Tis a poor man that doesn't know his own limits an' failings. But 'twas always like that, an' always will be. There's no changing people.'

He was about to walk out through them when Fionn stopped him.

'One minute now, Taoscán, before you go. Sure, we have no notion what happened to that lad inside, or why.

Are you going to leave us here in ... in the darkness of our ignorance? Are you?'

Taoscán looked him in the eye and smiled briefly.

'Come up out of this cold place, up to the hall, an' I'll tell ye whatever ye need or want to know – after I consult my secret book. There's something at the back of my mind that's bothering me.'

Fifteen minutes later they were seated edgily above, chilled in spite of the great fire blazing, yet every one of them peppering to hear the story.

THEY HAD BEEN FIFTEEN minutes of frenzied activity that Taoscán spent in his cave-workshop, though none of those who greeted him so excitedly when he returned could have known that, so calmly did he enter. But it was a ploy learned by him over years of dealing with cases of this type, necessary when breaking news of the Other World to simple men of this one.

He had gone straight to his black-covered book of secrets, opened it and flicked the calfskin leaves impatiently aside until he came to the place marked Cumhacht. His eyes had darted along the lines of ancient letters, looking for the clue he needed. And ... there it was! His forefinger tapped the spot in satisfaction and he drank in the wisdom of the words, nodding silent agreement as he read.

'The smoke,' he breathed. 'Of course! What else?'

He had turned, reached up and taken from the back corner of a high shelf a tiny jar. He had pulled out the stopper, shaken a pinch of a white powder into his left hand, frowned and then carefully replaced the jar. It was his precious vision-powder, a last resort in extreme cases, the druids' advantage over ordinary people, their means of knowing the unknowable.

He had moved to the hearth, sprinkled the powder onto the glowing turf-embers and watched intently. A wisp of white smoke had curled up, then several more, mingling as they rose to form a pale, wavering curtain. Shapes had begun to appear then, one after another, more and more rapidly, as if life itself was hurrying across a screen. And not a single one of them had escaped Taoscán's notice.

If his heart was shocked by what he saw, or saddened, or gladdened, never a sign of it showed on his grizzled face; he had seen too much in the course of his long life to be surprised by anything now. He had merely stared until the last of the smoke faded, then closed the door swiftly behind him and climbed the Hill, meditating on how best to explain what he had just witnessed.

LÚBÁN, THE HALF-CRIPPLED DOORKEEPER, had scarcely pulled the door of the hall behind Taoscán when a hundred pairs of eyes were fixed on him, a hundred necks straining in his direction. Yet, no word was spoken until Cormac rose and cried – 'Aha! You're come back at last, are you? Sit up here, man, near me an' give us all the news from the Other Side.'

He chuckled at this little nugget of humour, but even Goll, that least witty of men, looked askance at him. How was it, he wondered, that their king, the most important man in Ireland (at least officially), could so often be found wanting on the big occasion? And it was clear that others were thinking the same thing, for men suddenly began to scrabble for their goblets and wolf down drink at an alarming rate. But if Cormac's manners were less than kingly, Taoscán's, as usual, rose to the challenge, and that merely by being himself. He flicked up his fingers in a little gesture of greeting, shuffled up the hall and settled himself in his usual place, to the right of the king's seat.

Cormac, imagining that he had begun well, was determined to keep his humour on display.

'I s'pose 'twas the dead lads you were talking to, as usual. They must have told you a few things that'd make our hair stand up, eh,' he continued loudly, throwing an exaggerated and knowing glance at Conán's bald sconce. That old warrior grinned dutifully, then turned away, clenching his fists until the knuckles showed white.

'As a matter of fact they didn't,' replied Taoscán evenly, making himself comfortable. 'But what I have discovered will surprise you, all the same.'

'How so? Explain yourself.'

Taoscán looked about him at the expectant faces.

'What I have to say must be said to everyone, your highness. And it is a story not easy to understand.' He raised his voice then. 'So listen well. I will repeat no part of it.'

A creaking of seats. Men leaned forward, heads in hands, ears cocked. He continued, 'I told ye about Draointeoir, didn't I, the man who could have been the chief druid of Ireland only for that cursed ambition of his?'

They nodded. 'You did.'

'Well, he's behind all this. An' in spite of everything I knew about him, it never dawned on me before this night that he has so much to answer for.'

These last words were spoken more for himself than for the company. But the company was in no mood to be denied.

'How's that? Tell us more.'

'He's gone down farther into the Evil Arts than anyone realised. When we lost sight of him we knew that he had no good wish for us, but none of us ever thought he'd try to take out his revenge on the whole world. But there 'tis – evil ambition again!'

'Hold on, there,' called Fionn. 'What d'you mean "the whole world"?'

'He's lurking beyond in that place called Thuringia, in the middle of a dark forest, working on a plan that'll put all the known world in his dirty grasp.'

'But how could he do that?' demanded Diarmaid. 'I can't believe anyone could be so stupid. Won't Lugh strike him down, if the worst comes to the worst?'

'That might be,' replied Taoscán mildly, 'but think of all the poor, innocent people who'll get injured or worse until that happens. The gods step in only when men – an' women – have failed seven times.'

'You might as well tell us what his plan is – if you know it,' rasped Cormac, far less inclined to humour now than he had been.

'Oh, I know it, all right,' nodded Taoscán. 'An' I have to admire it, in spite of the badness that's in it. Great thought went into it, whatever else.' There was regret in his voice as he said it, then added more softly, 'But I'd expect no less from one who served his time with the druids of Ireland.'

'None of that oul' hugger-mugger, Taoscán,' bawled Cormac. 'Tell out what you know now, an' no more about it.'

Taoscán raised his voice.

'He's painting a picture. The Picture of the World he's calling it. With the help of it he means to have power over all things under the sun. As simple as that.'

'If that's what you call simple I'm a head of cabbage,' snorted Cormac.

Taoscán looked at him as if he might be willing to concede that point and then added, 'I'm only giving the barest notion of what he's at, but if ye want to know it all I'll tell it, though 'tis the kind of thing that might be better off not told.'

'We want to know!' roared a hundred voices and the tables trembled as fists thumped to emphasise the point.

'Settle, so, an' listen.'

Only when he had complete silence did he continue.

'This Picture of the World needs one thing above all others: faces. I'll explain the why of that in a minute. But to get the faces he had to train seven assistants in certain of his own skills. An' I can tell you, he had no shortage of people looking to join him in his evil work. But the people of Thuringia were always strange like that. Living in gloomy forests, cut off from all great learning, they wanted to prove to themselves an' to the whole world that they were people of high civilisation. Then, as if all their hopes an' wishes were being answered, a man of great skills comes among them, speaking their language! 'Twas Draointeoir, of course, an' he blinded 'em with his sweet tongue, his spells an' promises of glory to come.'

'Hold on, Taoscán.' Fionn was on his feet now. 'Is it any harm to ask what has all this to do with the faces? I don't see how the two things are connected. Hadn't he plenty of faces there in Thuringia ... or whatever you call the place ... if that's what his madness wanted?'

'Ah, but no,' replied Taoscán patiently. 'No. They would not do at all. With them he'd only have power over Thuringia, an' sure, he already had that. What was necessary to make his picture complete was three faces from every nation in the known world. Only so would he gain power over *all* peoples, an' once he had 'em all in his picture he could make 'em do whatever he wanted.'

He paused to allow this to seep into his listeners' minds and then continued: 'You see, that picture he was painting 'em into, as soon as 'twas finished they'd be trapped into doing whatever actions he had 'em doing there, an' that for as long ever as the picture was in existence, no matter what their own wishes might be.'

Frowns and scratchings showed men trying to grapple with the very idea of this.

Cormac shifted uneasily.

'You mean to say that if he painted me into that picture as a stealer of cows, that's what I'd find myself doing for the rest of my life?'

'Worse than that, your highness,' intoned Taoscán. 'Not just for your lifetime, but maybe for ever an' a day. As long as Draointeoir wished. But there's one vital other thing necessary, remember. In order to make you do that he had to have an exact picture of your face. That's why he sent out his seven assistants – to bring back the faces that he needed.'

Cormac's jaw dropped as the full meaning of Taoscán's words began to dawn on him. He snatched his goblet, golloped down a draught of poitín, then wiped his lips nervously.

'Go on! Go on!'

'At the end of all, Draointeoir would rule the world with his picture. An' why?'

Heads shook, unknowing.

'Because he'd get the ones he had power over to destroy any he couldn't control.'

Fionn summoned his voice. 'But ... surely you don't mean to say that the people in that picture are *alive*?'

''Tis a kind of half-life,' replied Taoscán. 'The same way the slua sí exist, there an' not there at the same time, if you understand me.'

They knew well enough what he was talking about. Liagán sat up suddenly, alert.

'But ... but why did he take the faces here that he did? What was important about Fergus, Garad, Sciabhrach an' Fearadach?'

'Good thinking, Liagán. Your head is clear this day, whatever else. An' I can answer that for you, too. You see, it wasn't just the faces of the mighty an' the powerful he was after. Kings an' warriors he had in plenty from the Great Sea to the edge of the Eastern World, but there was something else – '

'Wait!' shouted Cormac, leaping to his feet. 'What d'you mean "plenty kings"? Are you trying to make little of royalty? 'Cos if you are –'

Taoscán was well prepared for such a predictable outburst.

'There's no insult at all to you or your brother-kings,' he soothed, 'an' when you hear what else I have to say you'll see why.'

Cormac sat, a sour look on his face, and Taoscán spoke on. 'The something else he needed to make his plans secure was the faces of three red-haired men of Ireland, because as everyone knows, there's no one nearer the Other World than them. If he was sure of them there was nothing to stand in his way. But all that is finished now. Ye have only to look at the mess of blood down in the Black Hole to know that much.'

Goll, who had not been heard from for a long while, now raised his voice.

'Is this the only country where his plans failed?'

'I won't know that for sure until I meet the druids of the Seven Lands at our next conference, but you can be assured that this will set Draointeoir back a long, long way. I'm dealing with spells an' magic for enough years

to know that much. By the time he has another appren-
tice trained to the same skills as that poor lad below, we'll
have a hardy surprise ready for him.'

FOR THE NEXT HOUR and more the hall buzzed with talk of
what Taoscán had told them, and the general feeling was
that the world had had a close escape and Ireland should
not be shy about announcing to all and sundry its part in
the great deed. If nothing else it would drive the people
of Thuringia frantic with envy and regret.

Attention then turned to the Black Hole, and it was
Cormac who raised the matter. Obviously he felt none
too secure having such a pit gaping dangerously close to
where he was sitting.

'Are we going to leave the place below as it is, or
close it up, Taoscán?' he asked, trying to sound uncon-
cerned. The druid did not answer at once, only leaned
back in his chair and closed his eyes as if trying to decide.
Goll saw his chance.

'I think it'd be the right thing to keep it open, exactly
the way it is. Let everyone see it – no, *force* 'em to see it.
That's a sure way to teach 'em respect for the laws.'

'Yerra, what are you babbling about, Goll?' sneered
Feardorcha. 'In a few days' time won't everything in the
hole be changed. All that blood'll be as dry as a stick, an'
gone black, an' won't the maggots an' ciarógs – not to
mind the rats – eat what's left of him?'

Goll was about to defend his plan when Diarmaid
broke in. 'Anyway, haven't we too much gold made already out of that same place – unlucky gold I'd call it.
Maybe we should dump the whole lot of it back in there
entirely an' seal it up tight once an' for all.'

Cormac scotched this idea at once.

'None of that kind of talk! Any place that ever had a

foundation of gold didn't last beyond the second generation. I remember my grandfather to tell me that, an' he was a man that knew all the ins an' outs of palace foundations, 'cos he destroyed enough of 'em in his time. But ... but ... let me think, now. There must be something we can do.' And he smiled his fat, plotter's smile.

'Maybe it might be no bad idea to close it up, all right – but without the gold. I'll make use of that for noble deeds an' honourable purposes, never fear.'

Goll was not prepared to let his idea – one of the few he had had that year – go without protest.

'I still think it'd be the finest thing of all to put a bit of terror an' respect into evildoers. Only put 'em in there with the remains of that painter an' there won't be much noise out of 'em after it – or any other like 'em, either. In fact, better again, if we put in one scoundrel an' let him die of the hunger there, couldn't we let it be known that that's the only feeding the next tenant'd get: the body of the lad there before him. That's what'd bring law an' order back to the land of Ireland.'

Taoscán listened to all these opinions, saw the merit in some, the prejudice in most, and said at last: 'There's only one way of settling this. What we'll do' – and it was obvious that he, at least, knew what would bring this interesting but pointless argument to an end – 'is to leave it as it is below. We won't fill it in. Better that it should remain for a future generation to discover it. It'll give 'em some notion of how we lived. But for safety's sake we'll close up the stairs, an' the door leading to the steps. By doing that, the threat of it can still be there, but no sight of it. An' on the door let it be written in letters of gold – an' in pictures, too, for those who can't read words ...'

Here he paused, stroking his beard while he considered.

'... Mmm ... Aha! I have it! 'Tis coming to me. Yes ... These are the words to be written.'

MacCleite, the royal scribe, snatched a quill from behind his ear, held it poised over a sheet of vellum, and listened carefully. So did everyone else.

Behind these stones and deep below
the powers of evil beauty glow.
He who ventures past this door
steps out of life, comes back no more.

There was a pause, in which the only sound to be heard was the scratching of MacCleite's pen. Men turned the words over in their mouths, found them to their liking, and suddenly burst out into a torrent of applause, clapping and stamping of feet, and thumping of tables. Taoscán blushed modestly, bent his head and smiled. When the noise had died down he got to his feet.

'Thank ye kindly, men, for that. Now, it isn't good poetry by any manner of means. Dúnlaing, our bard, will tell ye that, I'm sure, an' all the reasons why. But if it serves its purpose an' keeps people away from the place below, I'll be happy enough.'

They nodded agreement, and Conán spoke for most of them when he sighed: 'Aw, Lord, isn't the bit of education a noble thing, too. How could we do without a man like that around the place?'

No one had anything more to add, and so what Taoscán recommended was done: the stairs filled in, the doorway closed up and built over, and the words of warning written there for the safety and instruction of all who might read them.

AND WHAT OF THE captain of the ship and his crew? They arrived at Tara a short time afterwards in a state of annoyance and agitation, for they had walked far on short rations, a state of things they were hardly accustomed to. They kicked the gates and made a general nuisance of themselves until they were at last admitted and allowed to explain their difficulty.

'My ship is ruined! She'll never again float. I want compensation, an' I want it now,' was the captain's quick summary.

'I haven't the first clue what you're talking about,' snapped Cormac. 'See Fionn MacCumhail. Maybe he'll be able to make some sense of what you're saying,' and he waved him from his presence impatiently.

'Who'd want to be a king?' he muttered, shaking his head, when they were gone. 'All the fools in the world seem to come to me with their stupid concerns.'

And he went off to his private chambers, refusing to see any more of his subjects for at least a week.

Luckily Fionn was in a better frame of mind.

'Dar fia, captain, I clean forgot about you!' he cried when the sailors were brought to him. 'An' you don't have to do any explaining. I know what has to be done.'

So saying, he picked out six of the Fianna and gave them brief orders: 'Help this good man to put his ship floating again. An' any damage that's done, undo it.'

They did that, and proof that they did their job well was the fact that the captain sailed that vessel to all parts of the known world over the next forty years with never a mishap, giving credit wherever he went to the legendary skills of the Fianna.

AND THE BLACK HOLE? And its secret? It is still there, deep under the sad, trampled ruins of Tara, waiting to be rediscovered, as Taoscán knew it would be. And on that lucky day the people of Ireland will again have a glimpse of what life – and a certain kind of death – was like in the far distant era of the High King Cormac and the Fianna of Éireann.

GLOSSARY

A dhuine: Informal greeting [My man]
Amadán: A foolish person
An slí díreach: The most direct way of doing something
Ar slí na fírinne: lit. 'on the way of the Truth', i.e., dead
Balor: Huge, evil-eyed, mythological tyrant
Bean feasa: A woman skilled in occult knowledge
Bodach: A rough ignorant person
Cailleach: A hag
Ciaróg: A black beetle
Ciaróg-doctor: A worker of evil magic
Conriocht: A werewolf
Cumhacht: Power
Dar an Tiarna Geal: By the Bright Lord [mild imprecation]
Dar fia: By the Lord [mild imprecation]
Dhera [Eng: 'yerra']: Interjection expressing indifference
Feallaire: A treacherous, untrustworthy person
Fiosrach: Inquisitive
Gimp: State or appearance of a person. Usually used with negative connotations.
Gruagach: An enchanter
Hugger-mugger [properly 'cogar mogar']: Whispering
In ainm Lugh: In the name of Lugh [mythical hero-god]
Lúbaire: A dishonest person
Óinseach: A foolish woman
Ollpiast: A serpent, a monster
Pádáiling: messing, acting in a purposeless way
Poitín: Strong liquor made from barley
Ráiméis: Nonsense, foolish talk
Scian: A knife
Searbhas: Bitterness, sourness of speech or attitude
Sleeveen: A person too clever for his own good
Slua sí: The fairy host
Snaidhm: A knot
Tuaiplis: Treachery
Uisce beatha [lit. 'the water of life']: Whiskey
Útamáiling: Groping, rooting
Wisha [Muise]: Interjection – 'indeed', 'well'